ROGUE LAW

The corrupt town of Montero wanted Julius Lang as marshal, but he refused the work as too dangerous and no job for an upright man. When persuasion didn't work, the town took Lang's ranch from him. And when pretty Matti Ullman arrived to lay claim to his land, Lang, needing to earn a living, was forced into the marshal's job. So Montero got Lang as their marshal — and they expected compliance — but what they got was rogue law . . .

LOGAN WINTERS

ROGUE LAW

Complete and Unabridged

LINFORD
Leicester

First published in Great Britain in 2008 by
Robert Hale Limited
London

First Linford Edition
published 2009
by arrangement with
Robert Hale Limited
London

British Library CIP Data

Winters, Logan.
    Rogue law- -(Linford western library)
    1. Western stories.
    2. Large type books.
    I. Title II. Series
    823.9'2–dc22

    ISBN 978–1–84782–701–2

Published by
F. A. Thorpe (Publishing)
Anstey, Leicestershire

Set by Words & Graphics Ltd.
Anstey, Leicestershire
Printed and bound in Great Britain by
T. J. International Ltd., Padstow, Cornwall

This book is printed on acid-free paper

1

Three .44 rounds were popped off nearby and Les Holloway untangled his legs and rose to his feet, reaching for his shotgun.

'Probably at the New Amsterdam.'

'Probably,' I agreed. 'I saw Cheyenne Baker and his crew riding in a couple of hours ago.'

'They've had plenty of time to get tanked up, then. Probably is them.'

We had been sitting in the town marshal's office, sipping bad black coffee and exchanging improbable stories. The shooting had interrupted that.

'Want to go along?' Les asked me, and I shook my head.

'I'm not the one the town is paying for that. Besides, Cheyenne doesn't like me and he might take the notion to extend his list of customers.'

1

'Nice sense of civic duty you have,' Les said sourly. He wasn't so much mad at me as at Cheyenne Baker and his gang for interrupting what had been up till then a peaceful Saturday morning. Les wore his badge uncertainly and didn't like having to stand for it unless it was absolutely necessary. He had a wife who was hoping that the job of town marshal would bring a tidy, steady income and give her the chance for a settled town life after grueling years of trying to scratch a living from a dry earth farm.

Les tucked his shotgun under his arm, touched his wildly bristling mustache and settled a glowering look on me as he walked to the door. I smiled in return, toasting him with my coffee mug.

I was still smiling when Les flung open the office door and stepped outside to be cut down by a swarm of bullets fired from across the street.

I dove for the floor with the .44s whining around the room, ricocheting off the brick walls, breaking the glass over the picture of President Grant hanging above the gunrack and nearly truncating my young and useless life. I found that a fragment of lead had nicked my elbow and, cursing the loss of my new yellow silk shirt, I crawled across the plank floor of the jailhouse as the bullets continued to fly. I saw two of them hit Les's prostrate body hard enough to cause him to lift slightly from the planks. I rolled to the side, away from the doorway and waited for the shooting to die down.

When the gunplay had ended I reached out, grabbed Les by his boots and tugged him into the office, closing the heavy oak door behind him. I dropped the bar across the door and crouched over Les. I hadn't expected to find any life lingering in him, and I did not. I crouched on my heels, silently, diligently cursing.

By the time I had Les placed on his jailhouse bunk, arms neatly folded, his face covered with a blanket, the

3

local citizens had started to arrive. Shaking their heads, murmuring platitudes, whispering regrets, they gathered in a tight bunch as if for protection. I sat with a fresh cup of coffee, my boots crossed on Les's desk and waited for the righteous anger to arise. That would be next after a few solemn moments, followed by the determination to rid the town of its bad element once and for all.

I said nothing to the solid citizens, saving my voice to instruct the mortician on what was to be done with Les. It was the same thing the town had done with its last three law officers — take him out to Boot Hill and plant him.

Righteous anger had faded and the mourning group of citizens reformed itself into a committee for action before anyone spoke directly to me.

'Lang,' the mayor, Calvin Jefferson, said after clearing his throat and hooking his thumbs into his vest pockets, 'we want you for town marshal. You're a man who can — '

'All right,' I agreed, causing a few eyebrows to arch. One of the women in the back tittered hysterically, but maybe she had thought of a good Irish joke.

'You'll do it?' the mayor asked, with a frown of astonishment, if such a thing can be formed on the human face.

'Yes. All I will require is a force of twenty deputies. These men will be available to work day and night, supervising all the gaming and drinking establishments in town. They will also be required to relieve all visitors of their firearms immediately they cross the city limits. Then — '

I made the mistake of taking a breath and the mayor jumped in. 'Impossible.' His hands flew wildly into the air.

'No more impossible than expecting one man to police these streets and alleys where dozens of armed drunks with imagined grudges and real disagreements are wandering.'

'What you are asking is absurd,' our town banker, a man named Rufus

Potter said, with a deep laugh. At least he found me amusing. The others, judging by their expressions, did not.

'No, sir,' I replied, 'what you are asking is absurd. As the ghosts of your last three town marshals would attest to.' I perched on the corner of the desk, my arms crossed. 'There is another way to convince me,' I told the gathered few. Their expressions brightened.

'Go on,' Rufus Potter encouraged.

'Is Judge Plank here? Good. As an alternative, the judge or someone else shall draw up a will for me. Now, the money — '

'What money?' Mayor Jefferson demanded.

'The five thousand dollars that you will insure my life for. This money can be paid to my mother upon my demise. She lives in St Joseph. I'll have to look up the address for you later.'

I had lost my audience. There was some angry muttering and a few loud disclaimers. I heard the woman titter again. That joke she remembered must have been a good one.

'Five thousand!' was all Banker Potter could force between his tightened lips.

'My life must be worth something,' I argued. 'You can't expect a man to accept a contract for suicide without having him think of those he must leave behind.'

'You're talking foolishness, Lang, and it's not amusing. Not at a time like this.'

'She thinks it is,' I said, having finally discovered the lady in green who was twirling a parasol, smiling and having a merry time considering it was a wake she was attending.

The mayor settled into a serious, man-to-man voice. 'Lang, you see that we need a peace officer. What is the town to do without a marshal? Every citizen has, must *feel* an obligation to his community. If we have not, we have no community.'

There was a group of kids in front of the jail, peering around the doorframe trying to get in on the excitement. I shooed them away with a sudden motion. I never have understood what fascination the dead have for people. Once a man is dead his entertainment value is pretty much nil. I was thinking that while the gathered committee thought I was considering obligations and such.

I rose from the desk and went to the hat tree to recover my Stetson. 'Gentlemen — and lady — I am not a citizen of Montero. I come in once a month or so to purchase coffee, sugar, salt, beans . . . tinned peaches or tomatoes, if McCormick has them at a good price, sometimes a few walnuts . . . which I recall now I forgot to ask for today.'

'Get to it, Lang!'

'And to see which of my former friends or acquaintances has been shot and killed because this town really doesn't give a damn about cleaning itself up except for hiring the occasional sacrificial badge-toter. Why is that? Because the town couldn't exist without its seamy establishments. What bunch of cowboys is going to ride in here on payday to watch the women knit socks or enjoy a checkers tournament? They want women, drink, card-playing and roughhouse.

'So do you all, though you won't admit it. The establishments you rail against are your tax base, your major bank depositors, your political backers. No — I'm sorry — I don't feel like pinning a bull's-eye over my heart and parading the streets of this hell town.' Another excited murmur began, but I hadn't come to argue with these people. I looked at the clock on the wall and announced that it was time for me to be riding. Stalking toward the door through a tunnel of angry gloom I heard a highpitched, musical voice call, 'Don't forget your walnuts!'

The lady laughed again. I guess I was even funnier than the Irish joke she had remembered.

The streets were dusty, white-hot and silent outside. I supposed that Cheyenne Baker and his crew had retired to the Golden Eagle to slug down a few drinks in fond remembrance of Les Holloway. I untied my little sorrel pony from the hitch rail and led it along with my pack horse back toward McCormick's Emporium. It wasn't only walnuts that I had forgotten. The morning's events had reminded me that it was time to stock up on ammunition. There had been a few rustlers slipping around my unfenced dry earth ranch lately. I had seen their sign, though I had lost but one calf, and that one may have just starved to death, considering the poor graze the Rafter L had to offer.

Yes, I had a registered brand though Les and others had thought it amusing that I would waste fifty dollars on the fees. Twenty-three (or two if that calf didn't show up again) cattle seemed hardly worth it to their way of thinking. I supposed I was amusing to a lot of people in many ways. I even nurtured hopes of making that dusty little pocket of New Mexico Territory into a real ranch with house and well and everything. No matter that I had been at it three years now and accomplished nothing but thinning what grass there was growing on the parcel.

'Your name is Julius Lang,' I heard the woman say, as I finished collecting my purchases from the counter in McCormick's store and turned to go.

'Lang will do,' I said to the woman in green.

'Lang, then,' she said, stepping nearer. I don't know if she could be called beautiful, but her lightly freckled face, her broad amused lips and steady blue eyes struck me as charming. The lilac scent she wore added to the charm and to my interest.

'Walnuts?' she asked, nodding at the small brown paper bag in my right hand.

'Yes. Want some?'

'They're out of season. If they're last year's they may be all black inside,' she said, 'I don't like them like that. Or full of dust the bugs left behind.'

'You're a connoisseur.'

'No, but I like them. Let's crack a few and see if they're any good. If they're all rotten, you can just toss them away here. Or maybe' — she inclined her head toward McCormick — 'he'll give you your money back.'

'Him! You haven't been in town long, have you?'

'No. Let's have a look at those walnuts,' she insisted, taking the bag from my hand.

So we sat outside on the wooden bench McCormick provided for his customers. There was a narrow band of shade falling across the plankwalk in front of the store. We cracked walnuts and talked.

Her name was Martha Ullman, but I was to call her Matti. She was from San Francisco and knew nothing of desert country although she had been born in Elko, Nevada. Uncle Webster Ullman was the one who knew this country — 'Hangdog' Ullman. Had I ever hear of him? No, I hadn't.

'I only arrived in town yesterday,'

Matti said. She was trying to crack a walnut with her teeth and I frowned and took it away from her, not wanting her to crack the porcelain. I managed the nut with thumb and forefinger and handed it back. She said, 'I slept for fifteen hours, got up and started for the courthouse and that's when the shooting began.'

'So, like any smart woman you jumped back in the hotel.'

'I went out to see what was going on,' she contradicted. 'That's when I saw everybody emerging from cover and storming to the marshal's office. I tagged along.' The next walnut she cracked beneath the heel of her little boot, smashing it flat. I retrieved another from the paper bag and did the honors again.

'There wasn't much to see, was there?' I commented.

'Just all those stuffed shirts trying to railroad you into doing something you didn't want to do and that they are afraid to do themselves. I laughed out loud. You heard me. I couldn't help it despite the fact that a man was lying there dead.'

'Les wouldn't have minded,' I told her. We had finished all the walnuts we wanted — only one of them had been black — and I rolled up the top of the bag and placed it aside.

'So,' she said, continuing her history, as we watched men and ladies, horses and buggies pass, the high-wheeled mine wagons stirring up clouds of yellow dust in their wakes. 'Uncle Ullman — '

'Hangdog.'

'That's right,' she nodded. 'Uncle Ullman passed away a year and a half ago. I didn't hear about it until recently. Our family is kind of spread out. Nothing much was doing in San Francisco — I had been trying to teach piano to a bunch of tone-deaf matrons and their bratty children.' She paused and corrected herself. 'No, the children were tone-deaf and the matrons were bratty.'

'Anyway,' I encouraged.

'Anyway,' Matti said, flicking a fly away from her forehead, 'it seems that Uncle Ullman left me a piece of property he had owned down here. A thousand acres less a county easement.'

'That's not a lot of land out here,' I commented.

'I know,' Matti said. Quoting, apparently, she added, 'Sere, inhospitable, sun-baked, waterless country where you can't grow rattlesnakes fifty to an acre, and they're considered to be prime stock down there.'

'You talked to someone who knows,' I had to agree. 'Then why bother to look at the property?'

'A person wants to see a piece of land if she owns it. It gives you a sense of belonging, if you know what I mean.' I said I thought I did. 'So here I am.' She let both hands flutter away, indicating Montero.

'Where is this property supposed to be?' I asked.

'I don't know exactly. That's why I

was going to the courthouse — to the land office to look at their plats. I have a general idea, that's all. Do you happen to know where Whipsaw Creek is?'

'I do,' I said.

'Well,' she said, lifting her eyes with the concentration of remembering, 'my property lies along Whipsaw Creek which I imagine is dry?' I nodded. 'And runs along it from the thirty-mile post all the way to Arapaho Peak. Does that mean anything to you?' Matti asked.

'Yes, it does,' I said carefully.

'Good!'

'Not good, Matti. The land you're describing is my land.'

'No,' she said quite calmly. 'It isn't. Hangdog, willed it to me.'

'*Hangdog* never owned it. That's the Rafter L you are describing. I ought to know, I live there.'

'You'll have to move, then,' Matti said. She was quite serious. The amusement had faded from her eyes.

'I will like hell,' I objected.

'I'm sorry, Julius Lang. You have a

nice enough face and your walnuts are just fine, but we cannot both be occupying the same parcel of land. I must ask you to leave. Of course,' she said generously, 'if you are running any stock, I'll give you time to clear them off my land. What will you require? A week? Ten days?'

'Come back in twenty years or so and ask me again,' I said, not heatedly but with growing resentment. She was as cute as she could be, but cocksure of herself. Was this why she had been shining up to me, or the reason she had been laughing at me earlier?

'I won't ask again,' Matti said, rising. She smoothed down her green skirt and picked up her parasol. 'I'll simply have the law — oh, that's right there is no law here now, is there? I'll simply have you displaced.'

'I'd like to see that day,' I said, rising to my feet as well. 'I don't know if you think this is an amusing game nor what institution you escaped from if you really believe what you're saying. Or,' I wondered suddenly, 'did somebody put you up to this?'

She unfurled her little green parasol, placed it over her shoulder and asked, without a hint of a smile, 'Would you like to accompany me, then, to the courthouse? Since you choose not to believe me, perhaps you will accept the fact of a legally filed deed and an inspection of the county surveyor's maps.'

Soberly, I nodded. Unlooping the reins to the sorrel and the dun pack horse from the hitchrail, I tugged down my hat against the glare of the sun and followed along — Matti on the plankwalk, me in the street, leading my animals.

'I miss the old times,' Matti said, after we had walked a way, her twirling her green parasol on her shoulder.

'The old times. San Francisco, you mean?' I asked hopefully. Maybe Matti had already had enough of this country and was thinking about going home.

She smiled and said, 'I mean the old

times when we were friends.'

'You mean when we would sit in front of McCormick's and eat walnuts without a care in the world.'

She nodded. 'Before you turned into a land-grabber.'

'Lady, I've had just about — '

She held up a dainty white hand, 'Save it, buster. We'll have this all resolved in a minute.' She lifted her chin toward the adobe brick courthouse half a block away.

'Buster,' I muttered under my breath.

She heard me and said, without turning her head, 'I can't call you 'Lang' any longer, can I? When we were friends, that sort of intimacy was all right. But now . . . '

I muttered something again. This time, fortunately, Matti did not catch it.

They stood square in the middle of the plankwalk and my jaw tightened with unhappy expectation. There were three of them: Cheyenne Baker, drunkenness marking his dark handsome features; the little man they called

19

Indio; Frank Short. Cheyenne's bravado was bolstered by whiskey, and possibly because he had shot down Les Halloway that morning. I had no proof of that, but here were the three of them and shots had been fired from three people when Les was gunned down stepping out of his office.

For whatever reason, Cheyenne was feeling all puffed up with himself. His hat was tugged low, his thumbs hooked in his gunbelt, his thin smile dirtier than usual.

'Well,' he said in a drawling voice, 'look at this little lady. Isn't she a perfect picture?'

I halted the sorrel, slipped my Winchester from its scabbard and stood behind my horse with the barrel of the rifle thrust across my saddle.

'Get out of the way, Cheyenne,' I told him, 'or I'll shoot you where you stand. All three of you.'

Glancing my way, he could see nothing but the sorrel, my eyes and the muzzle of the Winchester leveled at him.

'I'm just having fun, Lang,' Cheyenne Baker said, with a laugh that had no fun in it.

'You won't be in about three seconds, Cheyenne. They tell me that dead is no fun at all.'

'You wouldn't — ' Cheyenne sputtered, but he was not so sure that I wouldn't. *I* wasn't so sure that I wouldn't. With some grumbling, a lot of cursing and a few hate-filled backward glances, the three men sauntered away, moving off slowly to show me that they weren't really afraid. The front sight of my Winchester followed them down the street until they crossed and entered the New Amsterdam again. Matti stood watching the episode with a veneer of amusement that didn't quite mask her apprehension.

'Rough town,' she said finally.

'Too rough for you,' I said, shoving my rifle roughly back into its scabbard. 'If I were you I'd think about taking the next coach back toward San Francisco.'

Her look said, 'You're not me,' and

21

she sashayed down the rest of the block, entering the courthouse. I hitched my horses again, glanced at the saloons across the street and followed her inside.

We sat together on a wooden bench, waiting for the clerk, Nathan Hanson, to come back from wherever he had gone, unspeaking for minutes, Matti thoughtfully twirling her parasol on its ferrule. Eventually, glancing at me, she said, 'I knew it! You do have what it takes to be the town marshal.' When my expression remained blank, she explained, 'The way you backed those three toughs down.'

'What brings that thought up?'

'You will be needing a job, won't you? Now that you no longer have a ranch. You might want to reconsider being the marshal here.'

My angry response did not rise to my lips.

'Were you protecting me?' she asked, pursuing the matter. 'Or was it that you think those men killed your friend?'

'I don't like them, that's all,' I said, glancing up as Hanson bustled in, banged the door closed and indicated that he would be with us shortly.

'I think it was a little of each,' Matti went on, wearing out the subject. 'You must have thought it over and regretted your decision not to take the opportunity to avenge your friend's murder.'

'When did I ever say that I wouldn't?'

'Well, you refused to wear a badge!'

'One thing has nothing to do with the other. I won't wear a badge for a bunch of people whose only interest is keeping *themselves* safe and comfortable while they're in bed with the very crowd that is the cause of their trouble.

'As for taking revenge for Les's murder, that's a different story,' I told her.

★   ★   ★

Nathan Hanson, his thin silver hair slicked back, bespectacled eyes eager, beckoned to us from behind his

23

polished counter. 'I'm ready for you now,' he said, 'Who's first, or . . . ?'

'We are together,' Matti said regretfully. Her human side was again submerged beneath her businesslike exterior. She rose and walked to the counter. I followed. From the little reticule she had been wearing around her wrist, she withdrew what appeared to be a deed — old, much-folded, yellow.

'I want this authenticated. I wish to see the county plat of this property. I believe it is on page 44B of your map book.'

'Let's look at the map first,' the clerk said, placing the deed aside. He pulled down a large blue-bound map book from the shelf and opened it . . . to page 44B where the Whipsaw Creek range was limned in minute detail with precisely drawn black lines of ink. Every dry wash, rise, canyon and hump of earth was meticulously marked out there. Whoever had drawn the map was a man who knew his business and was obsessed with detail. From it I could almost visualize the country as it actually lay.

'Now, for this,' the clerk was saying as he unfolded the yellow deed Matti had brought along. 'What was it you wished to know, exactly?' he asked, thumbing his spectacles higher up the bridge of his nose.

'Just if that is the property recorded on this deed,' Matti said, her fingertip thumping the yellowed document, 'and if the deed is absolutely legal and authentic.'

The little man's ears went up as he concentrated. He bent lower over the deed, flicked at a seal with his fingernail, glanced at me and then at Matti and answered, 'Yes.' he concluded. 'And yes.'

The shooting began in the street before I could snatch up the deed and examine it for myself.

2

'Durn them!' the county clerk shouted, as he dove for the floor behind the counter. I grabbed Matti by the shoulder and took her to the floor with me as two shots and then another two rang out from in front of or near the New Amsterdam Saloon. We landed roughly. Matti complained in words that were muffled by her position, then held still as I forced her to stay down. After a few minutes of silence, we all rose, dusting ourselves off.

'Is this going to be an everyday thing?' the clerk demanded of no one in particular. 'We need some law in this town.'

'There's an opening,' Matti said.

I had eased over to the curtained window, but peering out I could see no damage done. 'I guess some of the boys just wanted to see if their guns still worked,' I commented, letting the curtain fall back into place.

'It's a hell town,' the clerk said without real passion. 'I'm going to request that my office be moved to a safer location.' From the way he said it I decided that it was an often-repeated complaint. If Matti had been shaken, she showed no signs of it now. It was back to business.

'Then everything is in order,' she said to the clerk. 'That is the property referred to on the deed and the deed is legal. The land is legally mine.'

The clerk looked again at the deed and nodded. 'If your name is Martha Jane Ullman.'

'It is,' Matti said, reclaiming the deed. I reached for it, but she folded it and put it way in her reticule before I could glance at it. The clerk was scratching his head.

'Ullman? No relation to Hangdog Ullman?'

'Yes,' Matti replied. 'He was my uncle.'

'You don't say!' the clerk smiled. 'I recall old Hangdog — '

I interrupted. There was heat rising to my face now. I wanted answers and I intended to get them. Something in my eyes must have spooked the clerk a little, for he glanced once at me and then gave me his full attention. I leaned across the counter, fists braced against the dark wood and spoke carefully and slowly to him.

'That land is mine,' I said between my teeth. 'I have the deed at home under a floorboard, but it was registered here.'

'That was wise, Mr Lang.'

'It's got a county seal stamped on it. Done by this office. When I bought that land from Henry Trent I had it witnessed by two other parties.'

'That was also wise,' the clerk said. Matti had edged away, not because she was worried about anything, but because she seemed to believe that her business had been completed and everything else was irrelevant. I caught a glimpse of her once, out of the corner of my eye. She seemed to be silently whistling a tune. The clerk was speaking:

'Before the deed was transferred, you did, of course, have a title search done?' he asked.

'A title search? No I did not.'

'That, Mr Lang, was *unwise*,' the clerk said, shaking his head sorrowfully.

'I had the deed!'

'More than one deed can be printed,' the clerk pointed out. 'As one who has been forced to deal frequently with disputed mining claims, I can tell you — '

'I know what I'm saying!' I said, containing my anger only with difficulty. 'Henry Trent held that land for a long time. I got the deed directly from him. I paid him one hundred and fifty dollars in gold money for that property.'

'So did someone else, it seems,' the clerk said. He removed his spectacles to clean them on his handkerchief. 'This is not infrequent, as I was about to point out — '

'There are witnesses!'

'You should bring Henry Trent here. A good lawyer could recover your money,' the clerk suggested.

'Henry Trent is dead!'

'Henry Trent sold that property to my Uncle Hangdog,' Matti said unhelpfully. 'Hangdog and Trent had the deed notarized and secured in Santa Fe. This was years before you thought that you had purchased the land. You were bilked. A title search would have shown you that your deed was no good.'

'You're crazy!' I said. She flinched a little as I raised my voice but soon got back to her whistling.

'All the evidence,' the clerk told me, 'bolsters the lady's position. The land seems to be hers.'

'You're crazy too,' I said, not so loudly as before. 'I even have a brand registered to the land.'

'You don't even need to have land to register a brand,' the clerk said uneasily. 'Anyone can register one.'

'You aren't listening. I have lived on

that land for three years. I built the cabin I live in on it, mucked out the well. I drove those cattle onto the land. It is my land!'

'You *do* need a lawyer,' the clerk said. 'If I were you — '

'You're not me,' I said. I spun on Matti again, 'Don't you have any cheap advice for me?'

'You'd better plan on moving your cattle unless you want to pay me grazing fees. I would consider that for the time being. It will be awhile before I can bring my own cattle onto the ranch. The cabin, whatever you call it, is an illegal improvement to my ranch. It also belongs to me. As for the rest,' — she gave a small feminine shrug, barely lifting her silk-clad shoulders — 'I am sorry you wasted all that time and effort, Mr Lang, but it is really all your own fault.

'My Uncle Hangdog was a scoundrel. In fact, they say that he killed a half-breed named Two Bob in Santa Fe and that was the reason he forever left

New Mexico. But one thing I will say for Uncle, he was always very, very careful in business matters.'

'I will sue,' I said carefully.

'I will be expecting a summons. Although I can't see how you can hope to prevail.'

I was burning with anger and there was some shame involved — shame concerning my own ignorance and stupidity. I wanted to yell some more, to curse, but I had shot my wad. Matti simply nodded to the clerk and walked out into the sunlight, unfurling her parasol once more. She was still standing there, waiting, when I exited half a minute later expecting her to be gone.

'I haven't eaten this morning,' she said, 'is there a decent place we can get a breakfast?'

I only stared. I couldn't think of a thing to say. Apparently, our little dispute now ended, Matti expected that she and I could go back to the 'old days' when we had been friends. Slowly

I calmed. There was no point in staying mad at her. She had won, it seemed, at least until I could find a lawyer, but how could I possibly pay one? She was smiling pleasantly at nothing, her green eyes as tranquil as ever, her face composed. She looked expectantly at me.

'The Coronet is a decent enough restaurant,' I said. 'It's right next to your hotel.'

Her eyebrows went up. *Surely*, they seemed to say, I was not expecting a lady to walk these streets unescorted and be forced to dine alone. And so I untied my horses and walked her down the street toward The Coronet.

★   ★   ★

Entering the restaurant which was small, cluttered with polished round tables and decorated with gilt and carved wood by Mrs Blount, the owner and cook, I paused to place my hat on the hat tree and followed Matti across the room to where one of the waitresses wearing a long white apron, her yellow hair pinned up high, offered a corner table to us. To Matti, that is. No one seemed to connect us. The waitress waited while Matti, sweeping her skirts aside, seated herself. The men scattered around the restaurant had their eyes fixed on her. I sat down across from Matti and folks seemed nearly shocked that this unshaven, lanky cowboy in his faded red shirt and worn blue jeans dared to sit near Miss Martha Ullman. The waitress hesitated before giving me a menu, then walked away, studying me oddly.

'I'll have the Spanish omelet,' Matti said, placing her menu aside. 'Now' — she folded her hands together on the table — 'we do have some business to discuss, Lang.'

'Can't it wait until after breakfast?' I moved my elbows from the table so that the waitress could put down a jug of coffee and two ceramic mugs. I looked up and said, 'Stack of hotcakes,' and the waitress frowned. I didn't get it, then I did. 'The lady will have the Spanish omelet. I'd like a stack of hotcakes. Please.' Matti was sitting there, looking at her empty coffee cup. It took me a while to get that as well, but finally a light dawned in my head and I poured her a cup.

'Now,' Matti said, daintily stirring a little sugar into her coffee, 'our unfinished business.'

'You'd better rein in your plans for awhile,' I said, 'until the court has had its say on matters.'

'That would put me behind schedule,' she said. I didn't know she had a schedule, but it figured that a woman like her would. 'First, I think you should stay on and work for me for the time being. I won't pay you any wages, of course; we can consider your work payment for your cattle grazing on the property. You will have to remove them when I am ready to move my own herd on. That's a month or so off,' she said, waving her hand to indicate that I needn't worry just yet. Matti had still another thought. 'You can help me with that, too, bringing my herd to the Whipsaw Range.'

'For free?' I said, giving the crazy woman the look she deserved.

'I don't know much about cattle ranching,' she said as if that explained things satisfactorily.

'Then *why*, Miss Ullman, are you even bothering? The matrons in San Francisco couldn't have been that bad! Why are you considering moving out onto that hardscrabble land where even experienced ranchers — '

'Like you.'

'Like myself, can barely make a living?' I studied her green eyes more carefully. They gave nothing away, but I wondered suddenly. 'Is it that you ran away, came down here, because you have something to hide? That you had to get out of San Francisco?'

'Do I have a shadowy past?' She let the waitress put the plates down. 'No, Lang. I do not. I simply made the decision, and when I make a decision . . . '

'I'm starting to get the idea on that,' I said, cutting a wedge away from the stack of hotcakes.

'Who is that?' Matti asked. I turned slightly. She was looking across the room, her eyes fixed on the tall man with the prematurely gray hair and narrow mustache dressed in a shiny blue suit. He was looking back with interest.

'Reg Kent,' I said.

'He's nice-looking.' She smiled across the room and I turned my head again, enough to see Kent return the smile. 'Who is he?' Matti asked.

'Your neighbor. Now. He owns the Hatchet outfit. He's a high-binder and a thief. Those men who were doing all the shooting this morning — Cheyenne Baker and his friends — work for Hatchet. You don't need to brand your cattle near his ranch, you need to tie them down.'

'Do they — Hatchet — rustle your cattle, Lang?'

'No, not *mine*,' I said, in a way I thought meaningful.

'If he is to be my neighbor, do you think I should introduce myself?' Matti asked.

'Why on earth would you bother to ask my opinion since you'll do whatever you please anyway? But, no, he's low and conniving. He'll smile while he's robbing you and some people like his smile so much they'll let him come back again for a second helping.'

'I suppose he runs a lot of cattle.'

'He does. Hatchet has good water in plentiful amounts. He's . . . obtained it over the years from the small ranchers along the Whipsaw.'

'I wonder if he would sell some steers to me,' Matti pondered, peering at Kent over the rim of her coffee cup. 'Otherwise stocking my ranch would involve a long drive, would it not?'

'It would,' I agreed — letting the part about it being 'her ranch' slide for the moment — 'but buying stock from somewhere else would save you the trouble you might have later when other ranchers start showing up to demand a closer look at your brands. Some people around here still look at buying stolen cattle as a criminal offense.'

'I'll have to ask some trustworthy people around town what they think,' Matti commented, showing me where I stood. 'With any luck,' she continued without taking a breath, 'my belongings should begin arriving on the afternoon coach.'

'Belongings?'

'Some more clothes, furniture for the house, utensils — you know.'

'You mean to furnish that shack?' I said with a laugh.

'You must have some furniture in it.'

'Sure. A cot, a table and two chairs. Matti, the place is little more than a hut thrown up to keep the weather off and the critters out.'

'I'll make do until I can add on or build a new house,' Matti said with a shrug.

'A new house? You talk as if you're

rolling in dough. A cattle herd, a new house!'

'I never said that all that Uncle Hangdog left me was that patch of land. As for the house,' she said, before I could make a remark, 'you will have a day and a half to remove your own possessions. You can throw up a lean-to or something, whatever you people do. Not too close to the main house, but not too far away. I'll need to be able to summon you concerning ranch business.'

'If you're thinking I would stay on to work for you, you're making a wild-eyed assumption, lady.'

'You have to watch your cattle, don't you? Have you another place to move them?' Matti went on. 'If they remain on my land — as we've discussed — I will have to charge you forage fees. I can't have your cows eating the grass my own will need gratis.'

I tried to interrupt, but she was unstoppable. 'Are there other hands on the ranch?'

40

'Only my man, Virgil Sly.'

'Two will be enough for now, I suppose. When I do bring my herd in, perhaps I can convince some of the drovers to stay on as ranch hands.'

'Why are you continuing to assume that I'll be a party to any of this!' I asked. My blood wasn't boiling, but it was simmering. My hands were shaking a little with subdued anger and I knew my face was flushed with temper.

'Because, Lang,' Matti said as she rose, 'you are in a tight spot. Unless you move your cattle off of my land tomorrow — which you can't do — they'll have to stay where they are for the time being. That means you have to pay me something for holding them. You are nearly broke, as you've as much as admitted to me. And,' she added with words that were like nails in my coffin, 'you have already refused the only work suitable for you around here.' She lifted an eyebrow. 'Unless you have decided that serving as town marshal would be preferable to working for me.'

'I don't know which would be worse,' I said, placing my napkin aside. 'I truly don't.'

She walked out then, leaving it to me to slide my last two silver dollars onto the table to pay for our breakfast. I hurried to catch up with her outside the door and, as I did, it occurred to me that I had been chasing her all around town that morning, following her like a puppy dog. I had decided I had had enough and was going to tell her so when she turned her green eyes on me, smiled and said, 'That's been about enough excitement for one morning. I'm returning to the hotel for a short rest.' Then Matti walked away, twirling her green parasol, smiling at the strangers she met.

★ ★ ★

My mood was dark and my thoughts savage as I headed the sorrel out onto the desert, leading my little dun pack horse. Half a mile on, I picked up the trail winding among the low-crowned, sage-studded hills that led toward the yellow-grass valley beyond where the Rafter L spread itself along the length of Whipsaw Creek, which was the dividing line between my land and Kent's Hatchet Ranch. Out of habit I watched for signs of interlopers, but, as I had hinted at when talking to Matti, Hatchet hands now gave me wide berth after that scrape a few years back where I — luckily — came out on top in a shootout with two Hatchet riders. I had sent them home over their saddles with a note to Reg Kent asking him please to respect our boundary line in the future. And they had, for the most part.

From the rim of the last rise I took measure of the poor cluster of structures I called my home ranch. The shack, tilting a little away from the prevailing western wind, two pole-and-brush outbuildings, the lean-to stable, the forty square-foot pole corral where just now Virgil Sly seemed to be standing around doing nothing at all but enjoying the day. It didn't even irritate me any more. I knew Virgil wasn't good for much except company, and we both knew that he took any time I was away from the ranch as being his signal to do even less than usual. I didn't pay him much, but he wasn't worth much. We agreed on that point and so we got along.

Watching me ride in, the narrow, hunched cowhand with the blue shirt torn out at the elbows placed one of his near-toothless smiles on his leather-colored face and lifted a hand in greeting. He took the lead rope to the dun as I swung down from my horse's back.

I stood still for a moment, looking up at the pale-blue sky. Nothing showed there, not a hawk or circling buzzard, not a wisp of cloud. Coming nearer, Sly asked, 'What are you looking at, Lang?'

'Nothing, Virgil. I just wanted to make sure the sky wasn't falling out here as well.'

'Something happen in town?' he

44

asked, as I uncinched my saddle and slipped it from the sorrel's back.

'Nothing much. They shot Les Holloway dead. Offered me the job of town marshal which I refused. Got my land taken away from me.'

I tossed my saddle over the sagging top rail of the corral and whipped off the sorrel's blanket, releasing it into the enclosure. Sly watched me as if waiting for the rest of the joke, a smile nearly developing as he watched with anxious eyes.

'What d'ya mean?' he managed to ask eventually. He fell in behind me as I tramped toward the house, carrying the sorrel's reins over my shoulder.

'Somebody showed up in Montero with a title to the ranch that seems to be better than mine. We've been given the option of working for them or drifting.'

I toed open the door to the shack, hung reins and bit on a rusty nail on the wall and sat down on a chair next to the rickety old table. Virgil Sly was trembling with excitement. He knew I wasn't joking. I never hold the punch line back that long. He removed his torn flop hat and scratched at his thin red-gray hair.

'A claim jumper?' He was incredulous. Probably because he, like I, hardly believed it would be worth anybody's effort to steal this patch of cactus-stippled dry land. Still, it was *ours*. Our only home.

Sly said, 'I'd like to see them try it. First sight I get of that claim jumper, I'll go to shooting.'

'I'll bet you wouldn't,' I said, winging my own hat across the room to settle on my bunk.

'Sure I would! Why wouldn't I?' Virgil Sly demanded. 'Of course I would,'

'No,' I told him, 'you wouldn't if you got a look at her.'

His look said it all — *a woman?* — a woman was going to try doing this to us?

I explained as well as I could as we started bringing the supplies in from the dun and stocking our miserable pantry. Virgil let me talk, not interrupting once although he made a series of doubtful, disbelieving sounds in his throat as I slammed our goods onto the sagging shelves and went on and on about the she-devil, Miss Martha Ullman, heartless destroyer of homes.

'What are you going to do, Lang? I mean, what are we going to do?' I was a long time answering; I had been a long time pondering it.

'The weather's holding fine,' I said at last. 'The horses don't need that lean-to. Clean it out and we'll move in there for the time being. 'I hope that it's not too close or too far from the house to suit her.'

There hadn't really been any choice as the lady had already figured out. I couldn't leave my cattle, the only real asset I had, nor did I have any place else to drive them. There was some free range in the area, but it was no more than blow sand where even nopal cactus withered and died trying to survive. I would have to stay on the ranch and work for Matti until I could find some way to prove up my title. Before leaving town I had stopped at the office of our only local lawyer, Bill Forsch, but he was not in. I had left a note sketchily explaining matters and saying I'd be back in a day or so to consult with him. I had not mentioned anything about legal fees, and though Bill and I got along well enough, I didn't figure he would see the profit in taking on a case without payment.

Still it was all that I could think of doing.

As I was raking the horse manure out of the lean-to, scattering fresh straw around for bedding. I told Sly, 'Well, this won't be too bad. We've both slept out under worse conditions.' Which was true, but that shack, this land had been purchased by the years of living like that, having nothing, saving every dollar that came my way while working for other people. Now, it seemed, I was right back where I had started from, and all because of some rich city girl's whim.

The city girl with the shiny red hair, charming smile, laughing green eyes and a taste for walnuts.

It was all too soon — I hadn't even gotten used to the idea let alone processed it. Yet at first light the next morning, with dawn still reddening the eastern sky above the long shadowed hills, here she came. Matti was alone. Sitting a big buckskin horse, wearing baggy black jeans, a man's yellow checked shirt and fawn-colored Stetson, she came riding directly toward the house while Sly and I stood bareheaded, stunned to silence, watching her arriving to take charge of the Rafter L.

3

Virgil had just emerged from the house where he had started the fire for coffee going in our old steel plate stove. He walked toward me, squinting against the light of the new sun, studying the incoming rider. There was a moment when he seemed not to believe what he was seeing, then his eyes focused on Matti and, when I glanced his way, I saw that his mouth was hanging open just a bit. His weather-lined nut brown face was fixed into a stunned trance-like expression.

'New boss?' he asked, when he recovered his speech.

'That's her,' I said unhappily. Why she had ridden all this way so early was beyond me. I suppose she was eager to mark her land. She seemed neither cheerful nor unhappy. There was a little half smile on her lips which could have meant anything. A few twists of her red hair had worked their way free of her Stetson and decorated her forehead.

'Good morning, Lang!' she said as she halted the buckskin horse she was riding. The animal looked too big for her. When she swung down, holding its reins, she barely came up to its shoulder. 'Virgil?' she asked pleasantly. Her smile melted Virgil Sly, striking him silent again. 'Will you please see to my horse for me?'

Virgil leaped forward as if no favor Matti asked could be too small or too large for him eagerly to perform. He didn't know her as I did yet.

Glancing at the smoke rising from the iron stovepipe, she asked me, 'Is breakfast ready?'

'Nothing but coffee,' I said with a half-apologetic shrug. 'That's all we usually do.'

'I'd like a cup. May I come in?'

'It's your house, isn't it?' I asked, with my resentment showing a little. She ignored it.

Virgil was falling over himself to assist her. 'Of course! Come on in. It'll be a pleasure to have an actual lady visit.' He blabbered on like that as he escorted her to the shack. I watched them enter through the door which was hung unevenly on leather hinges. Looking at the forlorn arrangement of buildings, feeling the rising breeze sweep dryly over my body I found myself wondering what I cared if I lost the whole place to this clever, charming little lady. Let her try to make a go of it out here.

It was all very fine to talk about driving a new herd onto the range, but the fact was that it could support no more cattle than I was running now. I had paid Henry Trent 150 gold dollars for my 1200 acres, and many were the times that I decided that old Henry Trent had gotten the better of the bargain.

I wandered over to the corral, still sunk in shadowed thoughts. The sorrel came over to me and I stroked its muzzle and sleek neck. I watched a coyote running in the low-tailed slink they have, dash across the far corner of the clearing, thought about shooting it, rejected the idea as being too much trouble and of little use. It was Matti's coyote now. Let her shoot it if she wanted to.

From nowhere, as I stood, boot propped up on the lowest rail of the corral, watching the skulking predator, a thought came to me.

I owned 1200 acres of this dry, barren land — or had, before yesterday. But Matti had told me that her deed showed that she had possession of 1000 acres. 'Minus a county easement,' she had added. A county easement was something they retained just in case some time in the next century they might decide to build a road or string telegraph wire or some such. A mere strip of land intended for such use should the county ever need it.

Where had the other 200 acres of land from my parcel gone to? I should have studied the map in the records office more closely. The sorrel nuzzled me for more attention, but my thoughts were elsewhere. In some way, for no reason I could fathom, 200 acres of land had vanished from my property. When selling to me, had Henry Trent held back a slice of land for his own later use, and let me go on assuming that the other 200 acres were included in my purchase? He had not made the same provision when selling the ranch to Hangdog, certainly. The acreage was defined as 1000, not 1200 on that deed, the one Matti held. Something did not make sense.

I needed to look at my original deed. Now.

I made my way to the shack and entered to find Matti and Virgil sipping coffee from tin cups, deep in a conversation. Virgil was saying: ' . . . 'Course since Lang here was acting marshal in Socorro, he managed to pull me out of what could have been a nasty situation.'

I glared at Virgil. He could talk about

himself all he wanted, but I didn't want him telling Matti about my past trails. She watched me over the rim of her coffee cup with amused eyes.

'I *knew* Lang must have been in law enforcement somewhere, sometime. The way they were so eager to press the marshal's job on him — '

'Move your chair!' I snapped, interrupting her.

'Pardon me?' she said, offended.

'Move your chair, Matti. Please!'

She rose, and the heavy chair was moved — by Virgil — and I removed the loose floorboard that covered my little cache beneath it. A brass box contained a record of my birth, a few other legal papers, twenty-seven dollars in silver money and the deed to this property signed by myself, Henry Trent and two saloon-bum witnesses. Crouching, I removed the deed, placed the box aside and opened the envelope containing the deed.

Sitting on my cot, I placed my hat aside and read the deed word for word, one at a time. Matti craned her neck, but she could see nothing from where she sat. Finished, I refolded the deed and placed it back in its envelope. Instead of putting it back in the metal box under the floorboards, I tucked the document inside my shirt.

'All right,' I asked Matti, before she could enquire where my concentration was, 'where did the other two hundred acres go?'

She looked at me blankly. 'I don't know what you mean.'

'Let me see your deed,' I said, extending a hand

'No.' Her refusal was flat and final.

'What two hundred acres?' Virgil asked, rousing himself from his soulful study of Matti's face.

'Miss Ullman here owns a thousand acres of land. Funny thing is, Virgil, I have a claim to twelve hundred acres, and according to the deeds, it is the same piece of property. I am asking her where the additional went. Where it was, as far as that goes.'

'I'm sure I don't know,' Matti said, as if nothing could matter less to her. She rose, tucked her red curls into the Stetson she was wearing and stood watching me, hands on hips. 'Is someone going to show me around the ranch?'

'I can't,' I complained, standing up. 'I don't even know where it begins and ends now.'

'You saw the map yesterday.'

'I wasn't looking for anything like that.'

'Lang,' she told me with a sad shake of her head, 'it seems that you are just not a very careful man.' I started to snap back, but she went on, 'If there is less land on my deed, then obviously either the former owner — this Henry Trent — decided that he did not wish to include it in the sale to Uncle . . . or Hangdog noticed the disparity and told Trent that there was a mistake which was then corrected. Uncle Hangdog — '

'Yes, I know,' I grumbled. 'Hangdog

57

was very careful when it came to business matters!'

'Exactly.' She turned her eyes on Virgil Sly. 'Will *you* ride out with me and show me the property.' Virgil was instantly ready to agree and was reaching for his flop hat before he thought to glance at me for permission.

'Go ahead,' I said sourly. 'She's the boss lady.'

'Then you are staying on?' Matti asked with one of her infuriating smiles. 'Both of you?'

'We're still here, aren't we?' I was standing now as well, as near to Matti as I could decently get, forcing her to lean back in order to look up at me. She didn't look in the least intimidated. 'I have some business to attend to in town,' I told her.

'Oh? Fine. We'll expect you when we see you,' she replied. Then she and Virgil started out the door, neither of them so much as glancing back as he began describing the lay of the land, doing all but strewing rose petals in front of her as they walked toward the corral.

I was still angry. Exactly what it was that made me maddest, I couldn't have said, or didn't want to admit. The minute they were gone I felt an odd loneliness creep over me. I stood in the doorway, watching as Virgil saddled his stocky blue roan, his mouth going a mile a minute. After a while they rode out toward the north, a cheerful laugh that had escaped Matti's lips lingering in the air.

★ ★ ★

It was Sunday morning and Montero lay silently baking in the harsh yellow sunlight. The Saturday-night roisterers were holed up asleep somewhere. The doors to the side-by-side saloons on Main Street — the New Amsterdam and the Golden Eagle — stood open, airing them out. The bartenders from each establishment, wearing white aprons, leaning on their brooms, stood in front of the businesses, jawing with each other. There had been a law passed some time ago to ban the sale of liquor on Sunday. Of course, the law was ignored.

McCormick's store was open, of course. The storekeeper never seemed even to catnap. One day he would die a very rich man. Just now he turned from washing his window to lift a hand to me as I passed.

I drew the sorrel up in front of Bill Forsch's office and swung down. It was Sunday, but Bill would be there. He had a small room over his office to sleep in. He said that he couldn't afford a house or even a room in the Western Hotel. I believed him. There really wasn't much call for a lawyer in Montero. Most of the people took care of their disputes without resort to a courtroom, finding it quicker and cheaper to do things their way. I found Bill's office door locked and proceeded to bang on it, thinking I could offer to buy him breakfast in lieu of a consulting fee.

After that I had no idea how I was going to pay him. From what I had gathered, resolving this matter was going to require a trip to Santa Fe and a few days of Bill's time.

Hair rumpled, wearing an unbuttoned vest over a half-buttoned shirt, the thin blond lawyer swung open the door. He wasn't angry, but neither was there joy on his features when he recognized me. He had a cold cigar clenched in his teeth and a vague, dreamy look in his watery blue eyes.

'Come in,' he said, there being nothing else he could say.

'Bill, I've got a problem.'

'I wouldn't have guessed it,' he said with soft irony. 'Take a seat and I'll tell you how much it will cost before you tell me you can't afford it and leave, having disrupted my morning routine.'

'I am sorry, Bill,' I said. I remained standing, just wanting to get matters settled. No matter how it turned out in the end. 'You got my note?'

'Yes,' he said, leaning back in his

chair, running his fingers through his untidy hair. 'I can't say it explained matters completely. Someone claims to have a prior deed to your land.'

'Yes, and it's odd, Bill,' I sat on the corner of his desk, watching him chew on his cigar and explained about the discrepancy between the size of the property on the two deeds.

'That is odd, I agree. If someone were simply trying to rob you of your property, why would they bother to work up a phoney deed with different boundaries than yours?'

'It does make you think, doesn't it, Bill? Doesn't it prove that something is up, even if I don't know exactly what it is?'

He remained thoughtful, looking at the ceiling as he moved his cigar around like a cow chewing its cud. 'Let's have another look at the county map,' he suggested. 'I have a spare key to their office. We'll check the corners and compare them with your deed. I don't suppose you know who originally surveyed the property.'

I shook my head. 'That would have been done ten years back or so. Henry Trent is gone, so unless there's a record somewhere . . . '

'There may be,' Bill said. 'In Santa Fe. For now let's have a look at the map. A shame you couldn't bring the other deed to compare yours with.'

'No chance of that,' I said. Bill was searching through his desk drawer and now came up with a brass key with a paper tag on it. He nodded and rose.

'Let's see what we can make of matters.'

The day was already warm when we traipsed out of his office and up the street to the county courthouse. Glancing at the saloons across the street I noticed three unfamiliar horses hitched in front of the Golden Eagle.

'New men in town?' I asked. Bill Forsch glanced that way and shrugged. He was chewing his cigar furiously, trying to get the key to work in the old lock. Finally it clicked and the door swung in. We entered the musty building, Bill going directly behind the counter to the case where the land maps stood neatly in their blue binders. He removed the one we needed to see.

Placing the book on the counter, he began thumbing through it. 'Map 44B,' I told him.

'That's what I thought,' the lawyer said, turning pages one way and the other as I watched anxiously, my deed in my hands. 'Lang?' Bill said after a minute. 'You're not going to like this, but I'm afraid . . . there is no page 44B in this book.'

'What are you talking about? Of course there is.' I pulled the book out from under his hands and turned it toward me, my face heating as my confusion rose. 'It was here yesterday. Probably two pages stuck together,' I said, my words rapid and sharp.

It wasn't there. The page was missing. Bill's finger pointed out a small uneven strip of paper stuck beneath the book's hinges. Page 44B had been torn out.

'Someone moved fast,' Bill said with a muffled whistle.

'The woman! It had to be, didn't it? She stayed in town overnight. This morning the page is missing.'

'Could have been anybody,' Bill said in a calming voice.

'No, Bill, it could not have been anybody! Who else would have any interest in that particular map page? Who else would have had access to it? Unless we are to suspect old Nathan Hanson who's had this job for twelve years and has no possible motive.'

'Maybe someone paid him to take it,' Bill suggested, but we both knew how improbable that was. Nathan would hardly risk his job for a bribe, and the two people who had any interest in examining the map — Matti and myself — had already seen it.

'She did it,' I said again, closing the book slowly.

'Why would she, Lang?' Bill Forsch asked me.

'I don't know!' I said in frustration. 'For the extra two hundred acres.'

'If they exist, she already owns them,' the lawyer pointed out, 'and if that was the point, she no longer has a map to prove they do or don't exist.'

'Then, Bill, you tell me? Who and why?'

'I've no idea, Lang. I'm no detective. I'm just a country lawyer.'

'As a lawyer, then, what course of action would you recommend now?'

'Same as previously, Lang. This can be cleared up by consulting the Territorial Record archives in Santa Fe. You know what that entails — two days' travel. Say a day and a half if I just happen to make connections. More likely two full days. Plus a day at the courthouse there. You'd need three full days of my time, plus I'd have to be paid for any lost fees I might incur by my absence. That begins to add up, Lang.'

I rubbed my forehead in angry disbelief. This could not be happening to me. The full force of my loss was only now beginning to settle on my shoulders. Bill was not trying to cheat me, I knew that. He was only telling me what I had already known.

'I don't suppose we could handle it by mail?' I enquired.

'If you know someone in Santa Fe who is reliable enough and knows his way around the courthouse — that would probably require another attorney, Lang. Besides, would you want to trust the result of such a search to the mails?'

'I am stuck!' I said, banging my fist down on the counter as Bill Forsch turned away to replace the blue book on its shelf. 'Good and stuck, and she knows it.'

'You still think it's the lady?' Bill asked.

'Who else?'

'I don't know, Lang. I do know from my past dealings with situations like this . . . people have been used as dupes before. Think about it. I don't know this woman at all; you do. Try to see her clearly enough to decide if she is really that sort.'

'You're saying that she might be someone else's puppet?'

'I'm saying as they do in court: don't be in a rush to convict.'

'I'll think it through. When I'm cooler.' I promised. We started again for the courthouse door. Stepping through, Bill said as he locked up again, 'Lang, if you can find a way to come up with the money . . . '

'I can't.'

'Well . . . I hope you understand,' he mumbled.

'I do, Bill. Truly.' I made a suggestion then. 'I owe you something for your time. How about if I buy you breakfast and promise not to discuss this while you're eating?'

Breakfast was enjoyable. As I had promised we talked no more about my case, restricting ourselves to conversations about the weather and those crooks in the legislature. We said goodbye in front of the restaurant and I watched Bill make his slow way back to his office. I untied my sorrel from the hitchrail and turned him homeward once again.

The day grew hotter beneath a white sun and I dragged plumes of yellow dust behind me as I walked my pony the length of Main Street. The riff-raff was up and beginning to congregate in the twin saloons. I spotted Indio standing at the open batwing doors of the New Amsterdam with a mug of beer in his hands. He gave me a sullen glance and turned his eyes away.

The three strange horses I had noted earlier were gone from in front of the Golden Eagle. Just passing through, whoever they were. I started homeward, the sun reflecting its brilliance from the desert sand into my burning eyes, the sorrel moving at a snail's pace which I did not object to. After all, where did I have to be, what did I have to do that morning?

The freight wagon was drawn up

beside my cabin and two men were trying to unload a heavy oak bureau from the tailgate. I heard one of them say to the other, 'All right, but you tell me where we're supposed to put it!'

Virgil Sly was sitting on the end of the sagging porch when I reached the house. He looked up at me and said, 'Don't bother trying to go in there, Lang. There's not a square foot of floor not taken up with the lady's belongings.'

'I'd forgotten she said that her things were arriving today.'

'They've arrived,' Virgil commented dryly. 'Some of them are stacked up on each other. I wanted a cup of coffee, but I couldn't even see the stove.'

'Well, at least we didn't have to unload the wagon.'

'There's that to be thankful for,' Virgil said, as I seated myself beside him. 'Say, Lang, I saw something that kind of mystified me this morning while I was showing the lady around the place.'

'Oh?' I scooted aside so that the movers could swing the bureau around and try wedging it through the door.

'The tracks of three horses,' Virgil told me, rising to his feet. 'Up near the Panhandle,' which was what we called an irregularly shaped patch of rugged land along our northern boundary.

'Hatchet riders?' I asked. Virgil shrugged.

'Had to be, didn't it? What they might have been doing up there I can't guess, though. All our cattle are bunched over near Arapaho. I counted them up. Still twenty-two head. I can't see Reg Kent sending his boys over for a picnic, so it's beyond me what they wanted.'

'Cheyenne Baker, Frank Short and Indio are still in town, so they haven't even been around.'

'Passing strangers, maybe,' Virgil said with a shrug. We both turned our heads as something inside the house fell with a crash. 'Though the Panhandle's well off the track for anyone just passing through.'

'Well off it,' I answered. I was thinking about the three strange horses I had seen in town earlier, wondering if there was a connection, and what it could possibly be. I supposed I should have taken the time to try to find out who those men were.

'Think Reg has hired some new hands, maybe?'

'What for? Round-up's a long way off and he's got all the men he needs now.'

'I don't know then,' Virgil said. He yawned and told me, 'I showed the tracks to the boss lady, but she didn't seem to take much interest in them.'

'I doubt she knows enough to keep her eyes open for range rats, Virgil. Anyway, let's us keep our eyes open because something funny is sure going on around here.'

I had not unsaddled my horse because I was busy considering, and considering brought me to thinking I would be happier riding out somewhere on the ranch than hanging around watching the lady's belongings be unloaded. I returned to the sorrel, and as it eyed me unhappily, I tightened my cinches again. Virgil had tagged along. He seemed distracted. His flop hat was tilted back showing his graying hair. His broad mouth was set. He seemed to want me to ask him a question, and so I did:

'What is it, Virgil?'

'Nothin', Lang.' His eyes told a different story as they dipped and shifted away.

'You had something you wanted to say.'

'Well, I did. But I don't think you want to hear it,' he said.

'Maybe not. Try me.'

'I was just thinking about everything. This trouble with your claim, the strange riders looking our land over. They might be connected, you know.'

'I thought of that.'

'Might have something to do with Reg Kent, too.'

'You're right again. Now suppose you tell me whatever it is that is on your mind, Virgil.'

'Just this — you could poke around, maybe find out what is going on. Where this lady comes from; if her deed is any good; who's trying to make trouble for us. Lang,' Virgil said with a sharp exhalation as if he were forcing himself to speak a callous truth.

'I reckon that if you were to become town marshall you would have the authority to look into matters and collect a few dollars while you were about it.'

4

I just stared at Virgil. Had he gone crazy; had the lady already gotten to him? 'You know I gave that up long ago, and you know why, Virgil. If I ever had to resort to that sort of work again, it sure wouldn't be in this town.'

Virgil was intimidated by my tone of voice and maybe by the gleam in my eyes. 'You ought to at least think it over, Lang . . . ' he muttered, before he turned away and started walking toward the house.

The two freighters had clambered back aboard their wagon and the driver turned the mule team as the swamper removed his hat to mop at his brow with a blue bandanna. The relief on both of their faces was obvious. They were pleased to be finished with that job. I lifted a hand to them as the rig rolled past behind the plodding mules.

I didn't even want to see the inside of the cabin just yet. I mounted my sorrel and rode out northward, toward the Panhandle where Virgil had seen the tracks of strange horses. There was nothing out that way. The land was mostly a ledge of solid rock, a few feet higher than the surrounding country. No grass grew and there were only spotty clumps of brush and cholla cactus. It was worthless for grazing and, as far as I knew, unremarkable in any way, which made us wonder why the three horsemen had paused there.

The day was pleasant enough. Hot, it was, but windless with a crystal sky. Walking my sorrel along the sandy trail through a stand of creosote brush, I startled a covey of quail and they scattered before the sorrel's hoofs, weaving their way toward safety, not frightened enough to take to wing.

I could smell water now, for there was water standing in isolated pools along Whipsaw Creek. For the most part, however, the Whipsaw was a broad sandy gully lined with dry willow brush and a few scattered, dismal cottonwood trees. If I hadn't smelled the water, I would have known I was near it by the surrounding presence of the swarm of gnats and the quick blue-gold darting dragonfly that whipped past my face like a tiny shooting star.

I looked ahead toward the low, broken hills someone had named Arapaho Peak, though this territory was far south of the usual range of that tribe of Indians. Maybe they had once roamed this land, I wouldn't know.

I couldn't get Virgil's words out of my mind. I didn't like the idea and so I had simply gotten angry, but he did have a point. I should at least consider the possibility. The job of marshal would give me a few advantages I did not now have, for instance.

I saw a chunk of leather fly from the pommel of my saddle, felt the sorrel flinch before I even recognized the sound of a rifle report. I didn't look around to see where the shot had come from. I leaped from leather, rolled into the brush and drew my Colt as a second shot echoed across the empty land. A third bullet searching the dry brush for flesh, furrowed the sandy soil a foot or so from my hand.

I lay hatless, sweat dripping into my eyes, Colt cocked and ready in my right hand, waiting. The shots had come from across the river, I thought. I searched the distances for a rising puff of smoke, watched for the moving shadow of a sniper or the silhouette of a picketed horse, but saw nothing.

Slow minutes passed without another sound, without movement as I studied the brushy bank of the dry creek. A stream of red ants had found my hand and decided to use it as a shortcut to their hill. I blew them off with a puff of breath and waited, squinting into the glare of the desert sunlight. I could see my sorrel, reins trailing, nibbling impassively at some mesquite beans it had found. I couldn't remain where I was indefinitely. Pinned down, my muscles already stiff, not an adversary but only a target for the marksman across the river.

I could not attack an unseen enemy and so I took the other option. Retreat.

I slithered forward on my elbows and knees, managing to stick to the clump of brittle brush long enough to reach my horse. I stretched out a hand for the reins and came up beside the sorrel, my pistol aimed eastward, eyes alert for any movement. There was none.

I turned my pony's head homeward and walked with it, staying behind the horse's shoulder for fifty yards or so before, risking it, I grabbed the saddle-horn and leaped aboard, heeling the sorrel sharply into a dead run.

No shots followed. No one cried out.

Angling through the brush I came to a narrow sandy wash, dipped into it, followed it a way then emerged on the far side. I was well away from the river now, screened by low hills, sagebrush and rocky ridges. Still I did not feel safe. When a man wants to shoot you, he'll generally find a way to pursue his idea.

What if it wasn't me in particular he wanted to kill? Maybe it was just anybody he saw. Would Virgil Sly's scalp have done just as well? Or Matti's! All this business with the conflicting deeds had gotten me thinking — maybe someone just wanted this land and was using anything that came to mind to obtain it, even murder.

Reg Kent. It had to be Kent, I thought. But why after all this time? He didn't like me, but we generally stayed out of each other's way, and he had no use for my dry patch of land that I could see. It was Reg who had all the good water, obtained by driving off or bullying the small ranchers farther north on the Whipsaw; Kent who had decent graze because of the water. So maybe I was doing Kent an injustice.

I put aside my intention of looking at my small herd of cattle to see how they were getting along, and headed my horse south again. Something more important than the cattle was on my mind now. I rode on grimly through the pale, heated light of the desert day.

★   ★   ★

I don't know who was more astonished to find me standing there when the door to Mayor Jefferson's fine white clapboard house opened to admit me — the mayor himself, Judge Plank or Reg Kent. All three of them wore suits, of course. Kent's was a pearly gray affair worn with a ribbon tie. His silver hair had a wave in the front and another where his mane disappeared behind his stiff white collar. The mayor wore a black suit as did Plank. The mayor's hair consisted of two white wings combed over his ears. Judge Plank couldn't boast that much plumage. His hair was vaguely orange, thin and fluffy as a gosling's.

I stood in the living room decorated with heavy dark-wood furnishings and waited for someone to speak. Two kids were playing a game on the floor near the fireplace. The little girl was in white, a big blue ribbon in her pale hair; the boy was dressed in a suit with short pants.

'I am surprised to see you, Lang,' the mayor said. He glanced at his other two guests. The judge's mouth was tightly pursed. Reg Kent was smiling as if he knew something I did not. A lot of things. 'Let's go into the other room,' he suggested.

We passed by an open door which led to a massive dining room. I could smell the Sunday roast cooking. I wondered if Reg Kent had brought the beef and to whom it had originally belonged.

We entered the mayor's private office where heavy dark-green drapes cut out the harsh glare of the lowering sun. The mayor closed the door behind us and seated himself behind his desk. Plank and Reg Kent took chairs. I remained standing. I wouldn't have wanted to soil the furnishings with trail dust.

'What bring you here, Lang?' the

mayor asked with wariness.

'I've decided to take the job of town marshal,' I answered, and for a long minute the only response was silence as the three men communicated with their eyes. I couldn't read the messages they were passing.

'This is a surprise,' Mayor Jefferson said cautiously. 'Yesterday when we offered it to you, you seemed to have no interest at all in the position.'

'I've changed my mind.'

'Of course we would have to consider — ' Judge Plank began. He never finished the sentence.

'What is there to consider?' the mayor asked. He glanced again at Kent. The rancher gave him a small nod. 'Lang's experienced, willing — '

'We can't rush into anything, Calvin,' Plank said nervously.

'Nothing will be different tomorrow,' the mayor responded. 'We still won't have a town marshal. Unless you know of someone?'

'No, no, it's not that,' Plank murmured.

He took a cigar from his vest pocket, toyed with it and put it away again.

'Kent?' the mayor asked.

'Have I a vote?' Reg Kent still wore that charming, humorless smile. He shrugged. 'I have no objection to Lang taking the job. Somebody has to do it. He's salty enough, and we know he can use a gun.'

I don't know what Kent meant by that remark. I let it slide.

'What would you require, Lang?' the mayor asked, his faded blue eyes now meeting mine directly. I told him.

'First, your authorization to do the job right,' I said. 'The town marshal has never been given a chance in Montero to make a real difference. There are too many privileged types running around. Men who see themselves as above the law.'

'That's a pretty general demand, Lang,' Judge Plank commented. 'What do you mean by 'authorization' exactly?'

'I want to know you're going to back me, Judge. Unless I know that, there's no sense in me — or anyone else — taking this job. If I am ever guilty of malfeasance, I expect to be fired. Let me do the job my own way and back me up: I can't do it otherwise.'

'I don't see — ' the judge began. The mayor cut him off again.

'Plank? You know the direction we want this town to take. We are more or less obligated to clean out some of our cobwebbed corners.'

Again unspoken messages passed among the three. I didn't care about that.

'Well?' I asked.

'We agree to those terms,' Mayor Jefferson said. 'What else will you require?'

'I'll need at least one deputy; I've got to sleep sometime.'

'Not Virgil Sly, I hope?' Reg Kent said.

'No, not Sly. He's got a job managing the Rafter L for Miss Ullman. I haven't got anyone in mind yet, but I will need someone to watch my back.'

'What else?' the judge asked uneasily.

'It's going to have to be made clear that discharging a firearm in town is a jailable offense. No exceptions,' I said, focusing my eyes on Kent.

'I assume you're referring to the incident involving Cheyenne Baker, Indio and Frank Short,' the cattleman said.

'I wouldn't characterize the murder of Les Holloway as an 'incident', Kent.'

'I don't know that they're responsible for that, and neither do you,' he said, his eyes challenging and cold. 'No matter — I've fired the three of them and after they've finished drinking up their wages, they'll no doubt drift down the road.'

That announcement seemed to surprise Judge Plank and Jefferson as much as it did me. There was no way of knowing if it was even true. You never did know with Reg Kent. The mayor wanted to wrap things up. Maybe the smell of that roast cooking was taking his mind in other directions.

'If everything is settled then,' Jefferson said, rising to his feet.

'It is,' I told him, 'except for one last point. I'll need some kind of line of credit with the bank.'

'I don't see . . . ' the mayor stuttered in confusion.

'The office won't run itself,' I said. 'The rest of you in city government have expenses, don't you? I need to have a source for petty cash, too. I'll need to stable and feed my horse. I'll need to eat. There are bound to be dozens of small items like printing notices and wanted posters, buying ammunition, meals for prisoners, janitorial work, fresh paint now and then, gunsmith's fees . . . any number of things. I can't be running to you, Mr Mayor, every time some incidental cost arises. I'll promise to itemize all expenses and submit receipts at the end of each month.'

'Lang's right,' the mayor agreed reluctantly. 'I'll set something up with Rufus Potter at the bank.'

'Is there anything else!' Judge Plank asked, more than slightly frustrated with me. I grinned at him.

'Just a badge and the keys to the jail.'

After I had put on my hat and had the heavy front door shut firmly behind me I stood congratulating myself. I watched the sunset as it painted the sky with wild colors and considered that I had pulled that off rather well. It did matter to me that I had now pinned the tin bull's eye on myself, but that couldn't be helped for the moment. Anyway, I had no idea of remaining town marshal any longer than it took for me to see my plans through. I swung onto the sorrel's back and started back toward town through the settling dusk. I wanted to have another meeting with Bill Forsch.

* * *

'You've got to be kidding,' was the lawyer's first reaction when I told him what I wanted.

'I'm dead serious, Bill. If I weren't, this would be a hell of a lot of trouble to go through for a joke.'

Forsch sat tilted back in his spring chair, cold cigar in his mouth. He rumpled his hair and attempted a smile. 'They'll hit the ceiling, you know.'

'I know it. When they get the bill — but that's not until the end of the month. By then I expect to be retired from the job as marshal. You just have your bags packed. I'll check with Potter at the bank in the morning to make sure the mayor has spoken to him about funding the marshal's office. You should be able to draw your money by then and catch the afternoon stage to Santa Fe.'

'Lang, they just won't stand for it,' Bill said worriedly.

'They will have no choice. They may not like it, but what can they do? Bill, they told me I was authorized to draw against town funds for valid expenses. Well, it seems to me that a part of my duties includes investigating suspected fraud.'

'Even when the victim is you.'

'I'm as much a citizen as anyone else. It's my duty to look into this land theft.' I wasn't able to maintain my solemn look. 'Withdraw what you require for stage fare and for your own expenses. As legal representative for the town government, you're authorized to do so.'

'You want me to compare the two deeds — yours and Miss Ullman's, discover if possible why your deed has two hundred more acres than hers, which two hundred they are, keep a sharp eye open for evidence of a fraudulent filing . . . anything else?' he asked.

'Check out that easement that's supposed to border the property. Find out where it actually runs. If you can locate them, find the original surveyor's maps, that might help as well.'

'All right, Lang,' the attorney said with a sigh. 'I don't know where this is all going to lead, but I know it's bound to take you deep into trouble.'

That was true, but what did I have

now but trouble? Displaced from my property, wearing a badge in a gun-crazy town. A pesky little woman kicking me out of my own house without so much as a thank you!

I closed Bill Forsch's office door behind me and stepped out into the purple hush of evening. The saloons were still quiet. It was early for the regular drunks to start getting their heads full of nonsense. I would just about have time to get over to the jailhouse and pin my badge on before whiskey-fused tempers started rising and the hell-raising began.

Or so I thought.

I would have to stable the sorrel, so I left it tied where it was and walked the short block to the jailhouse. Four strides on I reached the alley between the two buildings. Five strides on I heard the man's voice.

'Hands up! Step back in here, Lang. You're in my sights.'

'Indio?' I guessed. I could not see his face in the shadows of the alley. I could, however, make out the gun in his fist.

'What did I tell you to do, Lang? Or do you want to take it right there?'

I didn't. Nor did I want to take it in the alley. I considered my options, draw on a man who had me covered, try to dive toward the corner of the building, outracing a bullet. Docilely obey Indio, getting closer to him, maybe finding out that his intentions weren't as murderous as they seemed.

I liked none of those options. With resignation I entered the oily-smelling alley and approached the little gunman. 'What do you want, Indio? A few dollars? I heard you got fired off Hatchet today.'

'That's news to me,' the small man with the slicked-back dark hair said, easing toward me. Starlight gleamed in his eyes and shone on the bright steel of his Colt revolver.

'Why don't you turn around for me, Lang?' Indio suggested coolly. I was still weighing options, still not coming up with a good one. I didn't relish the possibility of a .44 slug tearing into my body, and at that range Indio would not miss. I hesitated and he repeated his demand.

'Turn around or I'll drill you where you stand.'

I thought he would have already done that if he was going to. I slowly turned, hands held high. In three steps he was to me, slipping my revolver from my holster. I heard it thud against the alley floor as he winged it aside. He wasn't finished. I felt his free hand patting my shirt and trouser pockets as the muzzle of the Colt remained jammed against the base of my spine.

'If you need a few dollars — '

'Shut up!' He continued to search me. Slowly it came to me. He was looking for the deed! With the map gone and my deed missing, I hadn't a leg to stand on. He couldn't know that Bill Forsch was now holding the deed. Indio was going to be frustrated in his search. Frustrated enough to shoot me where I stood? I knew he had no conscience and a bad temper. And I could smell raw whiskey on his breath. It was a bad combination. His right hand held the pistol. His left was busy frisking me. I couldn't wait.

I spun to my left, my left hand coming around to slap the muzzle of his pistol up and away from me as I grabbed his wrist with my right hand. The revolver discharged over my shoulder, the bullet whipping past within inches of my skull.

My nostrils were filled with gun-smoke. I tried my best to break Indio's arm, bending it back on itself at the elbow. He screamed in a high-pitched voice. I drove my knee up between his legs and he made another, deep tortured sound and went to his knees as I ripped the Colt from his hand.

Kneeling in front of me he clutched his groin, looking up at me with angry, savage eyes. He opened his mouth to curse me and I slammed my fist against his ear, sending him toppling to the filthy earth. A muttered curse came from his lips as he tried to rise.

Taking hold of his belt in back, I yanked him up into a crouch. I dragged him to the head of the alley. He pawed at the earth with boot toes and the heels of his hands, but I kept him moving. A few men, drawn by the shot, had emerged from the Golden Eagle Saloon to watch. They jeered and catcalled at Indio as I dog-walked him along the boardwalk toward the jail.

Kicking the door open, I dragged Indio into the marshal's office, crossed the room with him still in tow, and threw him roughly into a cell. Taking the ring of keys from the peg on the wall I turned the lock and stepped away to watch, hands on hips, breathing deeply as Indio crawled to the iron bunk pulled himself to his feet and turned to spit curses at me.

I walked to the desk, removed the marshal's badge from the top drawer and pinned it on my torn shirt.

I was officially open for business.

5

With Indio's pistol shoved behind my belt I walked back to the alley and retrieved my own revolver. Back in the office I took the time to clean and oil the Colt. Indio's gun I unloaded and shoved away in one of the lower desk drawers.

'I need a doctor!' Indio complained from his cell. He was hanging onto the bars, head pressed against them, dark hair falling across his eyes. There was blood trickling from his ear, but I saw no other obvious wounds. If I had it probably would have made little difference. I ignored him.

I checked the action on my reassembled Colt and holstered it. Taking a yellow pad of paper from the desk I licked a pencil and began writing.

'I need a doctor, Lang!' Indio said again. I didn't bother to glance up this time. He watched me with silent curiosity for a time as I labored over my writing and finally asked, 'What is that you're doing?'

I leaned back in the chair, holding the writing pad up. Without looking at him, I replied, 'Toting up the charges I'm going to lodge against you.'

'We got in a scuffle, that's all,' he said with a disparaging snort. 'What's that, a ten-dollar fine? Kent will have me out in half an hour.'

'No bond,' I said, placing the pad on the desk. I squared it and placed the pencil away.

'What the hell do you mean, no bond?' Indio demanded.

'Can't do it,' I said. 'Not with these offenses. Get used to stone walls, Indio. They're all you're going to be seeing for a lot of years.'

'You're crazy!' the little gunman said, but there was a quaver in his voice. Then: 'They'll bust me out, Lang.'

'Who? I already told you that Kent has cut you loose. I saw him tonight and he made that statement in front of the mayor and Judge Plank.' I paused and retrieved the pencil. 'You are now unemployed. I'd better add that — 'vagrancy'.'

After a long minute Indio asked in a calmer voice, 'What all have you got writ down there, Lang?'

'I guess you have the right to know.' I picked up the yellow pad and read to him: 'Armed robbery. Assault. Assault on an officer of the law. Attempted murder. Drunk in public. Discharging a firearm within the city limits. Vagrancy . . . I'll probably come up with a few other things if I consider long enough.'

There was a stunned silence from the jail cell. I got up and checked the wood in the potbelly stove and started a fire to boil some coffee.

'I didn't know you were a lawman then, Lang,' Indio complained.

'Too bad.'

'What you're talking about . . . if Judge Plank wants to make it tough on me . . . '

'Oh, he will,' I promised Indio. 'The town has suddenly got itself on a law-and-order track. I don't know why, but that's where they're taking their position now. You can't count on Kent to put a word in for you either. He was at that meeting at the mayor's house, and your former boss is supporting me just like the others.'

'But I mean . . . ' Indio began again. The firelight through the stove grate revealed a few beads of perspiration standing on his forehead. 'If the judge finds me guilty of all that, Lang, what could I get?'

'They won't hang you,' I said in mock consolation. 'The frame of mind the town is in, the judge is in, they'll be wanting to make an example of someone. You. I would guess you'll probably get twenty years . . . '

'Twenty!'

'Of course, that attempted murder could jack that up. No more thirty-five to forty, though.' I nodded and leaned back in my chair. The coffee had begun to boil. 'Say thirty years, Indio. I hear some men have survived that long in the Territorial Prison. A few . . . it's that hard-labor on the desert that gets most of 'em in five years or less. So if you were to get lucky . . . '

'Damn you to hell, Lang!' Indio spat. Then he decided to try wheedling. 'You could put in a word for me,' he suggested with feeble hope. I laughed out loud.

'I'm the injured party, Indio! Arresting officer and witness! Besides,' I added more quietly, 'I don't like you, Indio. Never have.'

From one of the saloons two gunshots rang out and I got heavily to my feet. 'What I can do,' I said, his face was briefly hopeful, 'what I can do, Indio, is walk across the street and find some company for you.'

The stars were bright. The street was empty except for two drifters dragging their way up Main Street. The porch in front of the Golden Eagle Saloon was empty — everyone had rushed back inside to see the excitement. Smoke rolled out over the top of the batwing doors. Some of it was tobacco smoke. I stepped up onto the porch, drew my gun, and eased up to the doors. From beside one of them I stretched out an arm and pushed, slipping into the clamor and stink of the saloon. The bartender looked up sharply. Men glanced at me and eased aside. The poker players around the round tables held their hands.

'Who's shooting?' I asked, just loudly enough for my voice to carry, and the mob separated a little more, enough to allow me a corridor of vision to the overturned table where Cheyenne Baker stood, pistol in hand, standing over a lanky, poorly dressed youth. 'Cheyenne, I've got to take you in,' I said. He had already seen the badge on my chest, but it didn't seem to surprise him. He only looked annoyed.

'Just a disagreement, Lang. I didn't even shoot him.'

'I've got to take you in,' I repeated,

striding nearer, my gun held level. His own Colt was dangling low beside his leg. His handsome face sneered without movement.

'Mind your own business, Lang.'

'I am.' I spoke loudly now, making the announcement without taking my eyes from Cheyenne Baker's. 'The posters haven't been hung yet, boys, but there's a new law in Montero. Anyone discharging a firearm in town will be jailed. I haven't decided for how long yet. I'm thinking it might mean ten days in the can.' I studied Cheyenne's cold eyes, the frightened eyes of the hayseed cowering on the floor. 'I might make it thirty days. We'll just have to see how quick everyone is to get the idea.

'Give me that pistol, Cheyenne,' I said. I knew he wouldn't turn his gun over to me. It wasn't only that he hated my guts, but he couldn't be seen to back down in front of the saloon crowd. If he happened to kill me and had to run — well, Hatchet had fired him and he would be drifting soon anyway. I could read all of that in his eyes, still I was a little surprised when he dropped to a knee and brought up the muzzle of his .44.

I shot him through the shoulder.

Either I had not had enough practice lately, or I was getting soft-hearted. I should have placed my slug where it would put Cheyenne out of his misery and me rid of him. But the .44 bullet tore into his shoulder just below the neck, passed through and thudded into the plastered wall behind him, sending Cheyenne Baker from his knees to his face, pistol clattering free.

'Pick that gun up for me,' I said to the dirt farmer Cheyenne had been bullying. My eyes searched the circle of men gathered near me, but no one was making a play. I spoke to two men I knew by name. 'Grant and . . . Eddie, tote that pile of meat over to the jailhouse for me.'

Remembering the third member of Cheyenne Baker's gang I asked, 'Where's

Frank Short?' No one spoke. Then, to the bartender, 'Where's Frank Short, Gus?'

'Haven't seen him, Lang,' Gus said, polishing a glass that didn't need polishing.

'If you run across him tell him that it would be a fine idea for him to just ride out of Montero and keep on going.' I spun back to Grant and Eddie who were standing by idly, their faces blank.

'I told you to carry this man out of here! Or you can leave him lying there to bleed to death if you'd rather, I don't really care.'

Cheyenne was writhing in pain, pawing at his damaged shoulder, but he did not make a sound as the two men picked him up, ankles and shoulders and carried him toward the front porch of the saloon. I backed out, my gun still leveled in the direction of the bunched men.

'Send someone to get Mama Fine,' I told the bartender as I eased through the batwing doors and started across the street, following the two men toting their bloody burden.

Indio leaped from his bunk as we entered. He gawked at Cheyenne Baker whose white shirt was a bloody mess and said, 'You don't waste time, do you, Lang? Going to clean up the whole town tonight?'

I ignored him and opened a second cell, watching as Grant and Eddie eased Cheyenne onto his bed. 'Is that all . . . Marshal?' the larger of the two, Grant, asked, sarcastically.

'That's all. Try to remember what I said over at The Golden Eagle, though. I've got two empty cells ready and waiting for anyone who forgets.'

In a display of sullen insouciance the two grinned at each other and sauntered out of the office. I didn't bother to lock Cheyenne's cell door. He wasn't going anywhere. Indio was again gripping the bars of his cell angrily.

'Are you going to let him die!'

'I sent for Mama Fine,' I told him, taking the boiling pot of coffee from the fire to let it cool for a minute before I poured myself a cup.

'That Apache! You're going to let her work on Cheyenne?' Indio bowed his head. 'Her and her potions and leeches and snake oil!'

'She's all this town has, Indio.' He knew it. We had once had a real doctor, but he did not much care for the atmosphere in Montero. Three months after he had arrived he was seen slipping aboard an eastbound stage. So all we now had in the way of a doctor was the medicine woman, Mama Fine. They said she was an Apache, but she didn't look it to me — her nose was too flat, her body too thick. Not that it mattered what she was. She sometimes managed to heal a man, but on the other hand — like a lot of *real* doctors — she didn't save them all. Of course when she succeeded it was taken for granted; when she failed it was because of her primitive ways.

I poured a cup of steaming coffee into a blue glazed cup and settled behind my desk, reaching for the yellow pad again. Indio kept watching me as if I were going to offer him a cup of coffee too. I didn't. I got to my scribbling instead.

The shadow in the doorway brought my head up. I was expecting to see Mama Fine standing there, but it was the kid whom that Cheyenne had been roughing up over at the saloon. I had completely forgotten about him — he was that kind of a man.

'I brought the pistol over,' he said hesitantly. 'The one you told me to pick up?'

'Put it on the desk,' I said. He looked more dazed than ever. Rail-thin, his oversized twill trousers were held up with suspenders. His red shirt was too big for him as well. His hair resembled a shock of straw. His blue eyes appeared childlike and world-weary at once. He placed Cheyenne Baker's gun gently on my desk.

'Pour yourself a cup of coffee,' I told the farm boy.

'Me?' he said hesitantly.

'You're the only one here. Stick around for a minute. I might need to ask you a few questions for my report.'

'What are you charging Cheyenne with?' Indio enquired sharply. I didn't lift my eyes when I answered.

'He drew down on me, Indio. You can't be shooting at the law. It looks like you two might be together for a long, long time. I told you I'd get you some company.'

'You just won't let up, will you, Lang?'

'Why should I? Now that you're coming in in bushels.'

Yesterday, I thought, I couldn't have done this. Yesterday Kent and his political friends would have been over here hollering and demanding the release of these two harmless fun-lovers I had heavy-handedly arrested. Yesterday I couldn't have gotten any of the concessions they had given me at the mayor's house. I frowned. What had changed since Saturday morning when Les was gunned down at the door of this very office?

Mama Fine wearing a long striped dress and a fringed shawl that looked like it was made of burlap waddled in carrying her medicine sack. I tilted my head toward the cell and she went in to see what she could do for Cheyenne Baker.

Yesterday morning I couldn't have gotten away with this. What had happened since then to change the attitude of the town bosses? Or, better yet, what *hadn't* happened? Matti had arrived, I'd found my deed challenged, land taken away, offered this job, refused it, taken it, got kicked out of my own house, been bushwhacked, had to arrest Indio after he seemed to be trying to steal my deed, shot Cheyenne Baker and laid down the law to the whole town about gunplay.

Wasn't that enough?

I looked up as Mama Fine's ministrations brought a pained groan from Cheyenne . . . Since Saturday morning. I had hired Bill Forsch to go to Santa

Fe to look into the disputed land title. Something else ... oh, yes. Three strange riders in town. Three strange horsemen moving around on the Panhandle. The same three? Who knew? Did it matter in the least?

I finished scribbling down Cheyenne's arrest report and shoved the pad aside. I tasted my coffee, found it already cold and rose to refill my cup. He was so quiet, so unobtrusive that I was startled when I rose, turned and found the scarecrow of a man still in my office, standing in the corner sipping at a cup of coffee.

'What's your name?' I asked him.

'Clarence Applewhite. Friends call me Cal.' His voice was so diffident as to be almost inaudible. I nodded and seated myself again, facing him.

'All right, Cal, suppose you tell me what happened in the saloon tonight.'

'Oh, I don't know,' he said reluctantly. 'I asked the bartender if I could maybe get a job there, mopping up in the mornings — Gus, is it? — Gus said he was too busy to talk just then and would I wait. So I went back to watch a poker game and this man — that one in there — said I stepped on his foot. I said I didn't think so, but I was sorry if I had, but he wouldn't accept that. I guess he was kind of drunk. He stood up and back-heeled me, knocking me down and when I looked up, he had a gun in his hand. He triggered off a round into the ceiling and told me to get out of there . . . that's about when you came in, I think.'

'Stupid things like that,' I muttered. Thinking it was things like that that got men shot, killed, or in prison. Cal looked at me, not understanding.

'I don't suppose Gus would hire me now,' he said ruefully.

'Need a job bad?' I asked and he nodded.

'House burned down. Daddy died fighting the fire.'

'Do you want to work for me?' I asked Cal, and Indio brayed a laugh from his cell.

'Do you mean it?' Cal asked uncertainly.

'Yes.'

'Well, sure! Of course. Anything at all.' He asked with increased caution, 'What do I have to do?'

'Run errands. Watch the jail when I'm gone. Tomorrow I'm getting some posters printed. You can tack those up around town.' I reached into the lowest drawer and took out Les's gunbelt and placed it on the desk top. 'Wear this.'

He picked it up and reluctantly strapped the gunbelt on. Indio snickered again at the sight of this pole-thin farmer wearing Les's big Colt, the belt tightened up to the last notch to keep it from falling down.

'Did you ever shoot a man?' I asked. Cal's answer was firm.

'No, sir! I have not.'

Indio thought that was funny too. I glanced toward the cell.

'You've hunted a lot.'

'Yes, sir. Deer, turkey, quail, dove with a shotgun, rabbits and such.'

'It's the same thing,' I said quietly. 'If you're more comfortable with a long gun, take that first Winchester on the rack.' It, too, was Les's weapon. 'Take care of those guns; they belonged to a good man. Have you got a horse, Cal?'

'No, sir.'

'See if you can find one you like at the stable tomorrow. The town will pay for it.'

Indio wasn't through talking yet. 'I thought you were crazy, Lang; I just didn't realize how far gone you were. Think the boys will back down when they see this deputy of yours brace them?'

I didn't bother to answer. I took a deputy's badge from the desk and slid it to Cal who pinned it on after studying its shine with a kind of awe for a minute. Mama Fine was finished with Cheyenne Baker, I saw. I walked over to look at him. There was a bandage wrapped around his shoulder and chest, holding the arm immobile. His face was chalk white, but calm-appearing. I let the medicine woman pass me and locked the cell door behind her.

'What do you usually get for a job like that?' I asked her.

'Two dollar. Two dollar,' she said, holding out a thick hand.

'I'll see that you get five. You have to come back tomorrow, though. After the bank is open, all right?'

She was used to cash on the barrel head and when she left she appeared a little disgusted with me, but I couldn't do anything about that. I told Cal to watch the jail while I went and stabled up my sorrel.

'Anybody tries to break in here, shoot 'em. If that bird in the cell, gives you any trouble,' I said, indicating Indio, 'shoot him.'

Later, when Cal had gone off to sleep in the loft at the stable and Indio had finally settled down, I turned the lamp wick down low and lay on the bunk where Les had died, watching the smoke from the lantern make eerie drifting shadows across the ceiling. I lay

114

awake a long time, reliving the hectic, crazy day, thinking about what tomorrow might bring.

And I wondered — for just a short hour or so — how Matti was sleeping on this warm, lonesome night.

★ ★ ★

I was at the bank before Rufus Potter had gotten there with his keys to open up the heavy mahogany door. I started to ask him, but he told me before I had finished my question.

'Yes, Lang — Mayor Jefferson has informed me. Just wait until one of my clerks arrives and we'll set up your account.'

It didn't take long, probably because Potter wanted me out of his way as quickly as possible. So, smiling, as the new sun rose, lost color and shrank in the flawless sky, I made my way to Bill Forsch's office to inform him that he was indeed bound for Santa Fe, courtesy of the town of Montero. I walked slowly back toward the office, feeling pleased with myself, jingling the walking-around pocket money I had drawn from the bank on my new account.

Somehow I had forgotten about Clarence Applewhite, but when I returned to the jailhouse, I found him outside, nervously guarding the door. 'Hope I wasn't late,' he said nervously. 'I know I'm supposed to watch the jail when you're gone.'

'No, everything's all right,' I said, unlocking the door. Indio was still on his bunk, but not sleeping. Cheyenne Baker had his eyes open, but he might have been asleep. It was hard to tell. His chest was rising and falling, however, so I supposed he was alive. I went to the desk and seated myself.

'Did you find a horse?' I asked Cal.

'The man there was showing me a bay pony. It seems sound, but he's asking quite a bit of money for it.'

'Buy it if you like it,' I told him. 'Have the stableman bill the town marshal's account. Also — buy yourself a hat, will you, Cal? After that get yourself some breakfast and bring back something for our prisoner and for me. Cheyenne doesn't look like he's going to be eating this morning, but we've got to keep Indio fed.

'Then,' I continued, 'I want you to go to the print shop and get fifty posters made up — I'll write down what I want them to say. You can pick them up later. After that come back here to hold things down while I look around the town a little.'

Cal looked pleased to have the assignments. I suppose it made him feel that I really did need him there and hadn't just offered the job out of pity.

'Say, Lang,' Indio said. He was sitting sleepily on the side of his bunk, rumpling his hair. His eyes shifted to me, 'How's about a cup of coffee?'

'Soon as I get it started. You'll need it. You are going to have a busy day, after all.' He looked at me blankly and I explained. 'I'm taking you to see the judge this morning. There's no sense in wasting time, is there?' He gave a small moan, anticipating what might be coming after he was brought up before Judge Plank.

I sent Cal on his way and started the fire in the stove going. That would heat up the office sooner than I liked, but I wasn't going to leave the door standing open. I needed no unexpected guests.

When Cal returned with a tray of boiled eggs, sliced ham and biscuits, we sat down to eat. I asked him what the printer had told him and if he had purchased that bay horse.

'The printer said he would have the posters ready by four or five o'clock,' Cal told me around a mouthful of food. 'As for the horse' — he shook his head unhappily — 'I told the stableman what you said about drawing from the marshal's account at the bank, but he looked at me as if I was a halfwit. Said he never heard of no such thing.'

'I'll talk to him,' I promised. 'I've got to go over and fetch my sorrel after a while anyway. Then I've got to try and catch up with the judge,' I said, glancing at Indio who was eating one hard-boiled egg after the other, popping them whole into his mouth. He took a moment to glare at me. 'Hope you don't mind, Cal,' I said, 'but you're going to have to spend most of the day locked down here.'

'That's what I hired on to do,' Cal said cheerfully.

I looked in on Cheyenne Baker. He had shifted position on his bunk, so I knew he was still alive. I'd have to talk to the judge about when we could have his trial. I took the time to warn Cal, 'If you hear any shooting out on the street, don't be rushing out to see what the trouble is. I've seen men killed when they were tricked into doing that.' Again I was looking at Indio. He knew what I meant. I would never find out for sure who had gunned down Les Holloway, but I would have bet anything that I had two of them in custody for other crimes right then.

119

Wandering over to Ike Kimball's stable, I retrieved my sorrel and began saddling while Ike watched me, his thick forearms draped over the stall partition. I had looked over the bay horse Cal wanted and agreed it was a good mount and that the price was a little high, but what did I care — it wasn't my money I was spending.

'So it'll be the same deal from now on?' big Ike was asking me. 'Stable fees, feed costs all get billed to the city.'

'That's right. For both horses. Just make up a bill daily, weekly, whatever you want and have me or Cal sign it. The bank will honor it.'

'Well,' Ike said, scratching his melon-shaped head, 'I guess that's all right then. The bank, at least I always know where it is. Some of these fellows that have tried to skin me by riding out when I ain't here I haven't found yet.'

'Ike?' I asked, as I slipped the sorrel its bit. 'There were three strangers passing through yesterday. They must have needed feed and water for their ponies. Did you see them?' I described the horses, but he shook his head.

'No. Maybe they went to Martinez's. If not there then they must be staying at a local ranch.' Like the Hatchet, maybe, I thought. I also wanted to know: 'How about Frank Short. Has he been around?'

'Frank? Yeah, he was in early this morning to pick up his paint pony. I heard him tell one of my boys that he was going to Santa Fe.'

Santa Fe? That could mean nothing at all. Frank was drifting now; why not head over to the big town? Still it was a coincidence considering that I was sending Bill Forsch out on the Santa Fe stage to check the legal records there. I convinced myself that it was only coincidence. No one could have known that the lawyer and I had discussed that plan.

Or could they?

I decided to warn Bill before he left so he would know that the possibility existed. After that I would see Judge

Plank and find out about walking Indio over to the courthouse to be arraigned. Then, if nothing was stirring in Montero, I meant to make a patrol of the surrounding countryside. I wanted to know what was happening up along the Whipsaw that would invite someone to take a potshot at me.

Maybe — if I had the time — I just might swing by the Rafter L. Find out if Virgil was making out OK. I might even — if I had the time — stop for a few minutes and talk to Matti. It was hard to escape the thought that somehow, knowingly or not, the little woman with the quirky personality and those big blue eyes was somehow at the center of things.

6

I was in and then I was out. One minute Judge Plank was pleased I was at the courthouse and, as I waited, Mayor Jefferson, also pleased to see me came in, shook my hand and disappeared into the judge's chambers. The next minute Plank's court clerk came up and told me that the judge was in an emergency session, he would be pleased to see me at a later time.

Shrugging, I rose, put on my hat and sauntered toward the courthouse door. I brushed past a tall stranger who wore a long dark flowing mustache. He assessed me with keen gray eyes, looked for a moment as if he would speak to me and then passed on. I saw the clerk wave him along to the judge's inner office. Apparently the stranger was involved in the emergency session, whatever it was about.

I sloughed off the snub. It was only a minor inconvenience. Indio was in no hurry to be arraigned, and he was secure where he was. I simply shuffled my schedule a little and decided that since I was now free of my obligations to the town, I might as well proceed to take care of my own.

There was an eerie silence across the land. It was clouding up a little, not much, but the wind was beginning to gust and crackle through the brush. I glanced northward, thinking that it might soon be raining dust. It didn't happen often, but now and then at this time of the year the weather shifted so that the north wind carrying thin clouds with it would drift across the desert and while scant rain was falling from the skies, sand was picked up by the stronger winds below and you would get a sort of a moist dust storm falling from the sky.

I passed two freight wagons, creaking slowly along across the yellow land. These at least were not carrying more of Matti's furniture to the Rafter L, but sawn lumber. I reined up at my turn-off to watch them, but they passed the Rafter L road and continued on. They had to be going to the Hatchet ranch, then. That figured — Reg Kent was the only rancher around who could afford such material. I had to wonder what he planned to do with all that wood, but I knew he would answer my questions about the time ice invaded the lower regions.

I found Matti on the front porch, broom in hand, industriously sweeping as if anything could keep dust from coating it again just as thickly within an hour. I wondered again why she, any woman, would wish to live out in this sorry corner of nowhere.

I didn't see Virgil around, and his little blue roan was missing from the corral, so he was probably upcountry, looking over the herd. My herd. If anyone was looking after them it should have been me. If anyone was crazy enough to sweep off the porch, that should have been me as well. It was my porch. My house. I waited until that little flare-up of anger subsided before I kneed the sorrel forward toward Matti.

I drew up and sat my pony, hands crossed on the pommel, watching her work. She did not glance up at me. Wearing a blue-checked calico dress and a white bandanna, she looked every bit the range wife — a very pretty range wife. When I had had enough of us ignoring each other, I spoke.

'Good morning, Matti.'

She turned, wiping her forehead with the back of her hand.

'Oh, it's you, Lang.'

'Yes, it's me. What are you trying to accomplish out here. Or is it that there's simply no room left for you inside the house?'

'I have all the room I need,' she shot back, 'and it's certainly much more comfortable in there than it was when you lived here. As for what I'm doing — I am trying to keep everything neat which is something else you could stand a lesson or two at.'

'Why so touchy?' I asked.

'You!' she said. 'Am I paying you to work here or not? Where have you been, Lang?'

She had not noticed the badge I was wearing so I tapped the silver shield and watched her expression change. 'I took your advice, Matti. Isn't that what you wanted me to do?'

She stepped toward me, one measured stride only, the broom held loosely in one hand. She tried to smile mockingly, gave that up and decided to look across my shoulder at the low clouds now beginning to settle over Arapaho Peak.

After watching her maneuver through so many layers of expression, searching for one that was meaningful, I decided that she could not answer the question I had asked because she did not know what she wanted at all. Perhaps not for me alone, but for herself as well.

'They told me — ' she said, and then her jaw clamped shut and she shook her head.

Frowning, I swung down from the sorrel and walked toward her. With one boot on the steps, I looked up and asked, 'What did they tell you, Matti?'

She shook her head again. Her eyes were still fixed on the approaching hard weather. Arapaho Peak had its head lost in the dark underbelly of the clouds, heavy shadows moved toward us as if pushed by the rising wind.

'Is it going to rain?' she asked me.

'Only a little,' I answered, not bothering to explain all about the unusual weather. 'Just enough to make you think it has.'

'Are you supposed to be here?' Matti asked.

'Do you mean can Montero get along without me?' I smiled lopsidedly. 'I would say that in general folks are happier there when I'm not around.'

'It's a rough town, isn't it?' she asked, and I thought I detected the barest hint of concern in her voice.

'Rough enough,' I agreed. I had been in more violent frontier towns, but there was a darkness about Montero. As if it bred a special sort of violence, the secret, stealthy kind. You could feel it in the air even if you could not see it. That, I thought, was something people like the town doctor who had just packed his bag and slipped away could sense about the town, the reason people didn't stay long or ever feel really comfortable there. There was nothing I could do to change that sort of evil.

'I felt a raindrop,' Matti said, 'you'd better come in until this blows over.'

It was the first time I had ever been invited into my own house, although when I entered the old cabin I saw that it didn't resemble my shack anymore. I looked at everything twice, my eyebrows drawing together as Matti walked to the stove and poured us each a cup of coffee.

There were curtains hung over both windows — two pairs. One sheer set next to the glass and heavier, brownish-orange drapes facing in. These were drawn back, cinched at the waist by velvet ropes of the same burnt-orange shade. There was a braided rug on the floor and on this two yellow plush sofas faced each other across a low oval table of dark wood. A vase with artificial flowers sat on it. Through the doorway to the bedroom I could see a made bed with a checked quilt, the corner of that heavy bureau with a mirror attached.

'Did you do this all yourself?' I asked, accepting a cup of coffee.

'The movers helped me shift some of the heavy pieces around. And Virgil helped me hang the drapes and roll out the carpet. He pretended that that sort of work was beneath him,' Matti said with a smile, 'but I think he liked doing it in a way.'

Of course he would, I reflected. Being around a woman like Matti, watching the grace of her movements, aware of the feminine scent of her, her eyes bright with pleasure as she found the perfect place for some item . . .

'Do you like it?' Matti asked me.

'It wouldn't be the way I'd have done it.'

She laughed, 'Well we *know* how you would do it!'

I smiled in return, but she wasn't exactly right. The way the cabin had been — well, it was like that because I was dirt poor and the money seemed better spent on other things. Besides, there had never been anyone around to fix things up for. The dusty rain was beginning to slap against the window panes and the walls of the cabin. It was darker outside and the driving wind set the cabin to trembling.

'Aren't you going to sit down?' Matti asked. She had a coffee cup — a tiny one — in one hand. With her other she patted the cushion of the yellow sofa.

'I'm not staying long,' I told her. I turned my back on her and watched the whip and swirl of the storm. Leaves from my lone oak tree scuttled and cartwheeled across the yard. 'Matti . . . what did they tell you? And who were they?'

Her eyes were innocent, but I thought her lip trembled a little as she sipped from her coffee cup. 'I don't understand what you mean, Lang.'

'Outside,' I reminded her. 'You said something about someone telling you something.'

'That's rather vague, isn't it?' She laughed again and replied, her eyes away from me, 'I really can't remember what I was going to say, Lang.'

I didn't prod her. We are all allowed our secrets. Only this secret seemed to concern me, and I didn't like being kept in the dark.

'The storm's already letting up,' I said, bending to peer out through the window. 'These things don't usually last long. I'm afraid you'll have to sweep your porch again, though. The wind just blew back everything you swept off.'

'That's the way things are out here, isn't it, Lang?' she asked, rising.

'Yes, I'm afraid so. Do you think you will ever get used to it, Matti?'

'I don't know, maybe not. But it doesn't matter if I do or don't. I am here to stay, Lang, and no one is going to run me off.' More sharply, she repeated, 'No one!' Her eyes were fierce; her hands had formed small, determined fists.

'No one's trying to, Matti,' I told her. 'I'll be going now . . .' I waited, but my words did not prompt a reply. She simply nodded and turned away. I opened the door and stepped out into the lingering shadows of the dying storm.

Virgil still had not returned. Probably he had sheltered up during the spate of rain and wind. That suited me just then. I wasn't in the mood to talk to Virgil or anyone else at the moment. I swung aboard my sorrel and waited a moment, glancing at the window to see if Matti was there, watching me go, but the curtains did not move, the door remained firmly closed. I heeled my horse a little too roughly and started the desolate ride back toward the diseased town of Montero.

Cal had been long alone in the jailhouse and his face flushed with pleasure when he unlocked the door and let me in.

'Anything happen?' I asked my thin deputy, replacing my Winchester in the rack.

'A man snuck up to the window and tried to hand Indio something through the bars.' I waited for the rest of it. 'I loosed off a bullet from my rifle and he changed his mind,' Cal said with a grin.

'Too bad you missed him,' I commented, settling behind my desk.

I told Cal that I had purchased the bay horse for him and, as he was so excited, I let him go off and try to find a saddle. A used one — my contribution to thrift.

About two o'clock I heard the snap of reins and the call of the stage-coach driver and I stepped outside to watch it begin its Santa Fe run. Bill Forsch was at the window on my side, his face dark with concern. I lifted a hand, but there was no response as the coach raced out of town, lost in its own dust cloud.

Closing the door I turned to find

Cheyenne Baker sitting up on his cot, holding his wounded shoulder with his good hand. His eyes were black embers when he lifted them to mine. He lowered his arm and flexed the fingers of his gun hand.

'You got me in the wrong arm. Lang,' he said, raising his right threateningly.

'Careless of me,' I said.

'I'll show you just how careless!' Cheyenne Baker roared, coming to his feet, though the sudden movement must have caused him pain. 'As soon as I'm out of here, Lang, you're dead. I'll be there standing over your grave to remind you just how careless you are.'

I sat in my chair, tilted back, hands resting easily on the wooden arms. I gave him a reckless smile and said, 'You're never getting out of here, Cheyenne. Only long enough to put on some chains and climb aboard the prison wagon.'

'Yeah, Indio's told me what you've been saying,' Cheyenne said in an ugly tone. 'Told me what you thought you heard.'

'I was there, Cheyenne. Kent said he was through with the three of you.'

Cheyenne Baker gave me a smile in return, every bit as challenging as my own. His voice was hoarse with emotion when he advised me, 'Don't believe everything you hear, Lang. You're playing a game you don't even understand. And one of the rules is that the loser dies.'

He had exhausted himself, it seemed, for he sat down on his bunk again and then lay back, staring at the ceiling. Indio continued to cling to the bars of his cell like an excited little ape, watching for my reaction. I didn't give him the satisfaction. I tilted back, propped my boots up on the desk and closed my eyes.

Maybe I had given no indication of it to the prisoners, but Cheyenne's words did give me pause for thought. Reg Kent had been quick to say that he had fired his three top hands, currying favor with the politicians, it seemed. Maybe Kent was just biding his time and there would be an attempted breakout when I least expected it. If he was going to do it, though, why not now? Before the two had been arraigned before Judge Plank? It wasn't a question I could solve, but I could make sure I was ready if anything did happen. I said nothing more to my prisoners, and they did not seem to be watching me when, after a few minutes, I rose, took a twelve-gauge shotgun from the gun rack and began cleaning it.

The passing storm had left the skies bathed in a lurid, blood-red light at sundown. The streets were silent as I walked them, alert for any trouble. I could still feel it in the air — this sense that something was hovering over Montero, ready to fall with a violent impact. Cal had posted the signs announcing the new ordinance here and there, and whether the law against discharging firearms was the cause or not, there was no rowdiness to speak of on this evening. I passed the alley between the courthouse and the feed store and caught two men in a fist fight, but they seemed evenly matched and equally drunk and so I let them proceed with their entertainment.

Glancing in the saloons I saw nothing riotous, but hostile eyes lifted as the men gathered there became aware of my presence. I stopped at the Coronet Restaurant to grab some supper. I couldn't take another meal in the jailhouse with Indio's remarks and Cheyenne Baker glowering at me. The waitress posted me at a corner table in the back of the restaurant and slapped a menu down before turning her back and strutting away. Two men at the front of the place who had not finished their plates pushed them aside, looked poisonously in my direction and went out.

My popularity continued to grow.

It was nothing new. A lawman is only popular with those he cozies up to. If it's not to their mutual benefit, the man with the star is the unwanted interloper, interfering with the natural right of the citizens to enjoy themselves and exploit their neighbors.

The waitress poured my coffee, spilling a little on the tablecloth. Another man got up to leave. A cook in the back dropped a pot and cursed.

And the guns exploded out on the streets of Montero.

I leaped to my feet, tipping the table. I threw my napkin aside and grabbed for my Winchester. No one made way for me as I rushed toward the front door of the restaurant. One man even tripped me — intentionally or not, I could not tell and could not pause to discuss. By the time I reached the plankwalk in front of the building, more than a dozen shots had been fired.

They came from the direction of the jail.

Men pushed their way through the doors of the saloons to crowd the porches. Others ran up the street to witness the battle. I fought my way past them, shouldering men aside. The next shot fired had the heavy report of a shotgun. Two pistol shots answered. They had the front door to the jail broken in, I saw now, and I jogged that way, levering a cartridge into the Winchester's breech.

I was spotted then. Three, four shots were fired in my direction and I flung myself aside, taking shelter behind the corner of the saddlery adjacent to the jailhouse. Bullets tore jagged splinters from the wall inches from my head. I ducked, tried to find a target, but had to withdraw again.

There was another flurry of shots and then a shout. I heard horses racing away up Main Street and took the chance. Rising, I stepped into the street and fired five shots after the retreating horsemen, working the lever of my rifle as rapidly as possible. I hit nothing. The horsemen never slowed their escape into the desert darkness.

A jeering cheer went up from the gathered crowd as I pushed a bullish man out of my way and raced on to the jail. It was worse than I had hoped. Beyond the shattered door I saw the two jail cell doors standing open

. . . and Cal lying face down in a pool of blood, shotgun in his limp fingers. A lone man had followed me to the jail and he now stood in the doorway gawking. I cursed and then shouted at him.

'Find Mama Fine! Make it quick!'

He hesitated fractionally, but then took to his heels as I lifted Cal by his shoulders and half-carried, half-dragged him into Indio's cell, placing the bleeding deputy onto the bunk vacated by the fleeing outlaw.

'There was too many of 'em, Marshal . . . ' Cal murmured.

I shushed him and cursed again, blaming myself. I had been given every warning that a breakout was in the offing. Cheyenne Baker had as much as told me so, and yet I had left the office to wander the town, even seated myself in a restaurant when I belonged here with the inexperienced Clarence Applewhite. The kid was nothing more than a displaced sodbuster, unused to situations like this, ill-equipped to handle them, and yet I had allowed him to guard the prisoners unassisted — probably the very situation the gang had been waiting for.

While I waited for Mama Fine, I filled the loops in a bandolier with cartridges and slung it across my shoulder. I took a box of twelve-gauge shells from the supply cabinet and a box of .44-.40s. I didn't know where I was riding, but I knew there was going to be a small war at the end of the trail.

I left Mama Fine laboring silently over Cal and walked toward the stable, a Winchester in one hand, shotgun in the other. My face must have looked as grim as I felt because the men in the street weren't slow in clearing a way for me now. I found Ike Kimball standing in the open double doorway to his stable and told him, 'I need somebody over at the jail. They shot Cal.'

'The kid? Is he all right?' Ike asked with genuine concern.

'He'll make it, I think. But I don't want him over there alone. Will you watch him for me, Ike?'

'What if they come back?' he asked, his wide forehead furrowing.

'Why would they? There's no reason for it. I just want someone there with Cal.'

'I don't know if . . . I've got things to tend to, Lang.'

I reached into my pocket. 'Ten dollars cash.'

'Maybe I could get one of my boys to do it,' Ike said, shifting the small gold coin from my palm into his pocket.

I was saddled and on my way out of town in minutes. The last color was gone from the sky, and out on the desert it would be black as a grave. There was no chance at all of finding the escaping men's tracks, and with the earlier rain, there would be no dust, not even a scent of it in the air to follow.

It made no difference. I would find them somehow.

I rode on into the heart of the vast, empty land. They should never have gunned the kid down.

7

After midnight the stars hung brilliantly clustered in the desert sky. The stray light they cast silvered the woody twigs of brush and illuminated scattered patches of drift sand so that they shone like mercury, but the desert trail remained dark and desolate, long-running and aimless.

I had thought first of the Hatchet Ranch when I trailed out after the gang, but they had passed Reg Kent's place by and headed out onto open desert in the direction of far-distant Socorro. Perhaps the outlaws knew of watering-holes hidden away in the folded hills out there, of tiny isolated pueblos where they could water their horses or trade them for new mounts. I did not. I was riding in the dark, mentally as well as physically, with the only light that from the angry fire burning within.

I thought now that Reg Kent had not broken his two men out of jail, but then just because they were riding away from his ranch did not mean he was not behind it. He wouldn't have wanted the responsibility laid at his doorstep.

Probably, I considered, the lid had come off in Montero now that the word had gotten around that I was gone and the town once again was lawless. I felt only vague responsibility for that. As I had told the citizens of Montero the day Les Holloway had been gunned down, they shared the blame for the state of the town. They had allowed the festering to continue, turning the other way unless the lawlessness directly affected their own prosperity.

The sorrel heard something. Or sensed it. I had been advancing at a walk to save its energy. Now I let it come to a halt. I watched as its ears twitched and it turned its head eastward. Could it have heard a distant horse nicker? Possibly there an animal scent in the air too faint for my own senses. On a hunch I started the sorrel forward, letting it have its head.

I did expect to come up on the outlaws sooner or later. Once they had put distance between themselves and the town, they would draw up weary horses and rest. They would have to. For one thing, Cheyenne Baker was in no condition to ride fast and hard. I, however, would not rest. They should have known me that well, but they did not.

For now, crowded together against a featureless sandstone ridge I saw the figures of at least three horses. I halted the sorrel again, watching, studying the night The faintest of breezes had risen, drifting light sand past at knee-level, carrying the pungent scent of creosote with it.

I heard a voice on the wind. Rather, a whisper. My mouth was tightened in a taut, grim smile. I shifted the shotgun I held across my saddlebow and walked my pony nearer, circling toward the low rise where the outlaws had sheltered.

I could still make out only three horses — one of them shifted its feet impatiently as I watched. They were still saddled, ready for a quick remount, and the horses didn't like it. Where were the others? There should have been six or seven riders. I considered that a few of the men might have participated only in the raid and then intended to slip back into town, the picture of innocence. It could also be that they were in the head-high brush beside the trail, just waiting for an easy shot at me.

I drew back the double hammers of the shotgun and continued forward.

I still saw only three horses. Three men. Which three? Maybe Cheyenne, wounded as he was, had needed to stop. Then, would Indio have remained behind with him? Likely. No matter — I would find out soon enough who was waiting for me in the night.

'Look out!' The voice seemed as loud as rolling thunder and one of the three men ahead of me leaped to his feet, opening up with a wildly aimed barrage of fire from his six-gun. Bending low across the withers, I heeled the sorrel hard, let it take a dozen long strides and cut loose with the scattergun.

Someone howled in agony and a second gunman went to the ground, firing up at me awkwardly as I reached the camp and touched off the second shotgun barrel. As it recoiled with a heavy jolt against my shoulder, I was already dragging my Colt out of leather, letting the shotgun fall where it may.

From his prone position, the outlaw with the rifle could not elevate the barrel of his weapon for a good shot. I winged two bullets from my .44 in his direction, not knowing if I struck him or not, but by then my sorrel was on top of him, and I rode him down, hearing the sickening sound of bone cracking. Ahead of me a third man was backed up against the sandstone bluff and I switched my sights to him.

'For God's sake, Lang,' he screamed, flinging his hands into the air, 'hold your fire! I surrender!'

I slowed and then halted my nervous, side-stepping horse, keeping my sights trained on the bandit who had given up.

'Where are the others?' I demanded.

'Gone. I swear it, Lang!'

By the glimmer of starlight I could now make out his face. It was Frank Short. So he had not gone to Santa Fe, but only told Ike Kimball that to cover his intentions. I swung down and marched deliberately toward Short. I glanced at the other two men. Neither was going to rise. Short was trembling. He had thrown his gun away.

'Who are they?' I demanded, nodding toward the dead men.

'The one you got with the shotgun was Brad Wilkie,' Short told me, mentioning a petty thief and gambler I knew vaguely. 'The other,' he said unhappily, 'that's Indio you rode down, Lang. You killed Indio dead.'

'If my deputy dies, you'll be dead as well, Short. I'll personally see that you're hanged for it.'

'I didn't shoot him! It was — '

'I don't care who did it! You'll all hang if he dies. Turn around, Frank.'

'What are you going to do?' His eyes were fearful white orbs in the starlight, his expression bleak as if he were already standing on the gallows.

'Turn around,' I repeated roughly. Then I checked him for a hideout gun and slipped his bowie knife from its sheath at the back of his belt, winging it away. I turned him around to face me and asked:

'Where's Cheyenne?'

'He couldn't make it, Lang. We left him in one of them old mine shacks up along Potrero.'

'Dying?'

'I don't know . . . he couldn't sit a saddle anymore.'

'So you just left him? You're a real friend, Frank. Where are the others?'

'They're townies. I talked them into helping me bust Indio and Cheyenne out. It wasn't hard to find men. They were eager to volunteer, saying it would serve you right.'

'Why'd you use townies? Couldn't Reg Kent spare any more men?' I asked.

'Kent didn't have a thing to do with it. I did it myself, Lang!' Frank said with a flush of pride. 'Planned it on my own.'

'You need to learn to plan better,' I said glancing at the dead men again. 'Unsaddle two of those horses, slip their bits and let them go. The Apaches can always use a few more ponies. Then you are riding back with me. You can tell me on the way who else was in on the jail break, or you can wait until you're locked up and I have the time to sweat it out of you.

'With luck,' I told him, glancing at the sky, 'we'll hit Montero by daybreak. Enjoy the free air tonight, Frank. You won't be seeing the sky again for a long time.'

★　★　★

There was a carpenter working on the front door of the jailhouse and about four men standing around supervising when I trailed up in front of the adobe building, a hint of red dawn still coloring the eastern sky, leading a somber Frank Short. Instead of gathering around to hear the gossip as you might expect, the onlookers backed away as I unloaded Short from his pony and steered him past the working man into the jail's interior.

One of Ike Kimball's sons — I couldn't tell which; he had four all pretty much identical — sat behind my desk, a rifle laid across it. He glanced up, seemingly unsurprised.

'How's Cal doing?' I asked reaching for the cell keys.

'He's better. Talked to me for a few minutes earlier.' He was reaching for his hat. 'I got to get back over to the stable, Marshal, if you can do without me for now.'

'All right,' I said across my shoulder as I unlocked the door to Frank Short's accommodation. 'Take my sorrel with you, it's worn to the nub. Might as well take Short's mount as well. Cool them down and grain them. Tell your father I'll need to borrow a fresh horse — Cal's bay will do. If he can spare you, or one of your brothers, bring the bay horse back over and watch the office again for awhile. The pay's the same, tell him.'

The kid nodded and went on his way, jamming a greasy hat on his head. I untied Frank Short and nudged him into the cell. The barred iron door swung shut and latched itself with that sound of finality that seemed to always puncture a bad man's bravado.

I looked in on Cal who was deep in sleep, not feverish. I hoped he would make it. It was my fault, after all, that he had been shot down. I mentally shrugged off the twinge of guilt and went to my desk, tossing the bandolier aside, and got down to business. I filled out most of a page on my yellow tablet covering Frank Short's charges and tossed the one with Indio's crimes into the waste basket.

Leaning back in my chair, hands behind my head, I stifled a yawn and let my eyelids slowly begin to drop. The rumble of a huge freight wagon stacked with new lumber moving past along the street brought me fully awake. The second one in two days. What were they doing with that much lumber? I walked to the door, eased past the carpenter and watched the massive wagon with its six-foot high wheels roll eastward.

Kimball's son was already returning, though he was not leading Cal's bay. I wondered at his eagerness, then remembered and reached for a ten-dollar gold piece. Ike would not pass up the opportunity to line his pockets.

It wasn't the same son, I saw, as he drew nearer. No matter, for my purposes they were inter-changeable. I asked the kid when he halted before me, 'Who's moving all that lumber?'

'That?' He looked toward their dust. 'Why that's a part of that Mr Alvin

Meredith's crew. We've been tending some of their horses.'

'Who is he?' I asked blankly.

'The big railroad man,' Kimball said, as if I were totally ignorant. It seemed that I was. What railroad? Who was Alvin Meredith?

'What is he up to?' I asked. I got an incredulous look in response.

'You mean you don't know . . . ? You can ask him yourself, Marshal. That's him there, going into the Coronet.' He pointed out the tall man with the flowing black mustache entering the restaurant. Where had I seen him? Oh, yes, in the courthouse attending the judge's 'emergency session'.

'Keep your eyes open,' I told the temporary deputy, giving him the ten-dollar gold piece. Then I stepped out onto the street and crossed to the Coronet. Something was going on. Something I should have been aware of long ago and intended to find out now.

Hostile eyes welcomed me as they had on my last visit. I paid no attention

155

to the faces, except to glance over them to look for the townies Frank Short had implicated in the prison break. But these, I guessed, would have taken to their heels, fled town at the first word of my return reached them.

Hatless, trail dusty, I walked across the wooden floor, boot-heels clicking, and seated myself without being invited across the table from Alvin Meredith. The man wore a nicely cut gray suit. His dark hair was just beginning to thin with middle age. His hands were narrow and white, but did not look weak. The third finger on his right hand was decorated with an emerald ring. Meredith lifted his gray eyes with a shadow of surprise as I scooted the wooden chair toward the table.

'Hello, Marshal Lang,' he said, touching his long black mustache with thumb and forefinger.

'You know who I am then.'

'You've been pointed out to me. And I know you by reputation,' he said easily. The waitress approached, but I waved her away. 'What can I do for you, Lang?'

'You can do what the important men in Montero won't. You can tell me what in hell is going on. What, exactly are you up to, Mr Meredith?'

He didn't like my manner, I could tell. I didn't care much for it myself, but I had been shot at, run ragged and had my land stolen from me over the course of a few days. My disposition wasn't the best.

Meredith narrowed his eyes a little and answered, 'The railhead, of course. I was sure that Judge Plank and Mayor Patterson had informed you of the details.'

'They haven't even given me the general outline,' I said, leaning my forearms on the table. 'What railhead, Mr Meredith?'

'The one we're building right now!' he said with mild disbelief. Did he think that I was pulling some sort of joke on him? He seemed genuinely astonished that I could not know what was happening in my own town.

I had a feeling, a knowledge really since it was the only thing that made any sense, of what he was going to reply to my next question, but I asked it anyway.

'Where?'

'Where is the construction?' His eyes remained narrowed. 'Along the easement. It's adjacent to the property that I believe you once owned. On a strip of land Reg Kent sold the railroad. Called, I believe — '

'The Panhandle,' I provided. The missing 200 acres. Somehow Reg Kent had ended up holding that land when the deeds were juggled.

'Yes, that's it,' Meredith agreed. 'It's the only suitable place along the easement for miles. Hard rock, a solid building foundation, unlike the sandy soil surrounding it.' He reached into his pocket. 'I have our new survey of the property with me. You might have seen our surveying crew out in the vicinity.'

I believed I had. The three strangers.

I told him, 'I don't need to see the map, Meredith. I know my own property.'

His hand halted halfway out of his pocket. 'What did you say?'

'I said The Panhandle is my land, not Reg Kent's. They wanted the railroad to come into Montero and they knew I wouldn't sell out. Knowing me, they also knew that I couldn't be moved off my land by force and so they concocted an elaborate scheme to steal it from me legally. To remove me they drew up a fake deed and gave the bulk of my property to a woman who is either a conspirator or plain gullible — I haven't decided which yet.

'That is, all of my land except for the two hundred or so acres fronting the easement, the only place along it where there is bedrock, a solid foundation for water tower, depot, warehouses, whatever you have planned to build. That, Kent somehow ended up with.'

Meredith's puzzlement slowly changed to defensive belligerence. I could understand that; he had been sent to do a job, thought he had completed it satisfactorily and now had me pop up in his path.

'Your suppositions are quite incredible, Lang,' he said softly, but not without malice. 'The mayor, Judge Plank, Reg Kent have all assured me that the railroad's purchase is absolutely binding, legally unassailable. I admit that I am a newcomer here — '

'That's right!' I said, so loudly that the heads of nearby diners turned our way. 'You are a newcomer to Montero. It's a rotten town, Meredith, filled with snakes and cunning, slinking predators.'

'Let's not descend to personalities,' Meredith said in a controlled voice. 'The facts are simple. Reg Kent had title to the land. He sold it to us. Assuming you ever did have a claim to that land, you lost it when the new owner of the Rafter L acquired the ranch. Tell me where I'm wrong?'

I wanted to spit. The man was right as far as it went. He wasn't finished.

'As a representative of the law, it is

your responsibility to uphold legal decisions, not to assail them on personal grounds,' the railroad man said.

'I was appointed marshal only to remove me from my property. Maybe they were planning to set me up to be gunned down in the streets of Montero. Maybe they really did want me to clean it up so that when the railroad big-shots toured the town it wouldn't wear its violent face and scare them off. Either way they would win.'

'If you don't want this job . . . I can always speak to the mayor.'

'You won't have to do that,' I told him. I unpinned the badge from my shirt and let it fall to the floor. 'I'm done with this town. All of it. I'll warn you, Meredith. Don't try to build on my property. And don't try to run me off: you don't have enough people for the job.'

'I think we might,' Meredith said smoothly, the threat behind his words obvious. 'This morning's newspaper will be out soon, a banner headline will announce to the town that the railroad is going to come to Montero. Just how many townspeople do you think will allow one man to stand in the way of progress?'

'I suppose we'll find out,' I said. I was at a loss for a better answer. I was holding deuces and the players across the table already had aces showing. I rose slowly, not angrily, but Meredith was a shrewd player and he knew that I was not ready to throw in my hand. I would run my bluff and see how the final cards played out.

I stepped on my badge as I rose, smiled and walked out past the vacant faces in the restaurant. I saddled the bay horse, the horse meant for Cal who might now never get the chance to ride it, turned its head eastward and rode from the town into the clean, open desert, shaking off the stink of Montero.

Matti and Virgil were both in front of the house when I reined up. Virgil noticed first that I was not riding the sorrel, Matti that no silver shield shone on my shirt.

'We got trouble, Lang,' Virgil Sly told me as I swung down.

'Do we?' I asked and Virgil frowned at my reaction which was only acceptance.

'Someone's building out on the Panhandle. Don't know who it is or what they think they're doing — '

'Ask Matti,' I said coldly. 'She can enlighten you.' There was no humor in my eyes and I received not a hint of a smile from Matti. 'Want some advice, Virgil? Make up your bedroll and pack your saddle-bags. Ride on out of here while you can. It's just going to get uglier.'

'Lang!' Virgil's expression was one of pained astonishment. 'How can you say something like that to me?'

'I said it because I care about you, Virgil.'

'I care about you too, Lang,' Virgil replied soberly, 'you and the Rafter L. Whatever trouble is coming, I'm sticking with you.'

Matti stood there, hands on hips, the breeze flattening her blue skirt against her legs and toying with her hair. She asked sharply, 'Don't you have any orders for me, Lang?'

'You do what you want, lady. But you should know that we might have half the town, drunk and angry, coming onto this property by afternoon. Nothing's going to stop them.'

Her voice was small, tight, breathless with determination. 'Oh, isn't it! I will stop them, Lang. I swear I will.'

She swept into the house. I glanced at Virgil who shrugged with his eyes.

'I'd better talk to her,' I said.

'I guess you had. What do you want me to do now?'

I gave him his instructions. He alternately grimaced, frowned and grinned. He went off toward the toolshed and I scraped off my boots on the porch before entering the little house where I found Matti standing at the south window, her clenched hands held rigidly at her sides.

'You need anything, Matti?' I asked

and she turned sharply to face me. There was glittering anger in her eyes.

'A gun! All I have is this foolish little .32 pistol.' She showed me a small revolver she had kept tucked in the pocket of her skirt.

'Sit down, Matti,' I said, in a tone I hoped she would not consider bossy. After a brief hesitation, she complied. 'You have to get away from the ranch,' I said, my eyes searching hers. 'I wasn't kidding about the danger you run here. Men will be coming up here, a lot of them and they will be angry and out of control.'

'I'll not leave. This is my land. No one has the right to push me off it,' she said in a brittle voice. She was angry, but far from hysterical.

'I see.' I paused for a moment. I had undervalued this woman, it seemed, mistaken her nerve and her determination. I had to ask. 'Matti, everything is coming apart now. Why don't you tell me how it really came about? What you are really doing here, how it came to pass.'

She took in a sharp breath, shook her head and then lowered her eyes. 'It doesn't matter any more now . . . if I tell you, does it?'

I said I couldn't see how.

'You asked me once if I have a shadowy background in San Francisco!' She laughed mirthlessly. 'I don't, Lang. I have nothing there. I *had* nothing there. The part about me trying to give music lessons was true — there just wasn't any money in it. Not enough to survive on. Maybe I wasn't any good at it, I don't know.

'My father was a sailing man and he vanished out on the Pacific. Mother, grieving, was in her grave within the year. I was left with nothing and I was ill-prepared to fend for myself. The promise of a new life appeared out of the blue when I was at my lowest point. An item in the newspaper placed there by someone searching for a possible heir to the estate of Webster Ullman also known as 'Hangdog' Ullman. A lawyer's address was given.

'New Mexico Territory! It seemed a desperate chance, but I was already two weeks behind in my rent and there was no promise of any employment on the horizon. I couldn't live on the streets. I grasped the opportunity desperately. When I arrived, one of the first people I met was already trying to take my only hope away.'

'Me.'

'You,' she answered. 'I wanted to like you, I did like you. But then the panic would return to me. What could I possibly do now, where could I go if not here? There was just nowhere left,' she said, explaining her mercurial moods, her stubbornness.

'I'm sorry, Matti,' I said, meaning it. 'If I had known — '

'If you had known, *what*? What could you have possibly done?'

'Understood a little more, maybe.'

'And after that? No, Lang, I began to have doubts about the true ownership of the ranch from the very first. Everything seemed suddenly suspicious. But

I had to cling to my claim of ownership, don't you see!'

'I do now.'

'Funny, isn't it?' She rose and went to the window, leaving the little pistol behind on the sofa cushion to gaze out at the stark form of Arapaho Peak. 'In the brief time I've been here, I've come to care about this land. I can't explain it. I know it's raw and dry and primitive. I couldn't explain it to anyone — it's like caring for a person no one else in the world likes at all. You just can't explain it. It makes no sense.'

'It does to me, Matti,' I said, walking up beside her to stand looking out across the long land of broken hills, desert flats, stunted mesquite trees and drought-deprived sage. 'This was my first home, too, the only place I've ever had to *belong*.'

She turned slowly to face me, looking up at me with determination. She clutched my sleeve with one small hand, clutched it very tightly and said, 'Then we will fight for our land, you and I, Lang. No one can run us off.'

'Just a minute,' I said. 'What I will do and what you must do are two different things. I have described what it will be like up here when the town arrives. Use your imagination and double whatever I've said. It will get ugly.' Her hand fell away at my rejection. The determination remained, however.

'I will fight, Lang,' she said with solidly spaced words. 'Where am I to go if I leave? If I let them drive me away? To Montero? And wouldn't that be a wonderful life? I am safer with you than alone anyway. No,' she shook her head definitely. 'I am here. I will fight for my land — and fight you for it later, if necessary.'

I went out onto the porch to leave Matti to change out of her dress. There was no use in arguing with the lady, and besides she did have a point. Where else was she to go? Virgil Sly was waiting nervously when I emerged from the cabin. I saw the canvas sacks he had tied on behind his blue roan's saddle.

169

'Anything else, Lang?' he asked.

'Saddle her buckskin,' I told him. He goggled at me for a second, then nodded and walked away toward the corral. In a minute Matti appeared wearing her black jeans and checked shirt. I was carrying two Winchesters, my own and another belonging to the marshal's department. I handed her one of the long guns wordlessly.

The sun was already fading by the time we reached that flat inhospitable section of the ranch we called the Panhandle. Nothing worth fighting over. Only a stony ledge of land skirting the lower reaches of the hills bordering the dry Whipsaw. It was nothing worth fighting for, nothing worth dying over. I had to remind myself that men had already died because of it, and that alone lent the Panhandle value. And to remember that there were men perfectly willing to kill me for ownership of this stony, barren patch of land.

From atop the low ridge we looked down across the Whipsaw at the

Hatchet Ranch beyond. Above us loomed the craggy Arapaho Peak, its shadow at this hour nearly reaching us where we sat our ponies. A slight breeze shifted the manes and tails of our horses. I surveyed the surrounding land and then let my gaze settle on the buildings below. We had heard the hammer blows, sharp and solid as gunshots and the rasp of saws long before we had emerged from the screen of brush to find the railroad crew hard at work on the skeleton of the railhead.

Sixteen men I made them at a rough count. Two heavy lumber wagons were centrally placed between twin buildings where the framers situated their beams. A dozen horses were ground-hitched near one of Whipsaw Creek's many cattail-encircled ponds.

'They may not fight,' I told the others hopefully. 'They have no stake in this except for their daily wages.'

'Men always protect what they have,' Virgil commented. 'It's built into us.'

'I don't see anyone wearing a

handgun,' Matti put in. 'There must be a few rifles around somewhere, but no one has one near at hand that I can see.'

'They're not expecting trouble,' I said, which was what I was counting on. And they were not fighting men, but hard-working laborers, focused on the job at hand.

It didn't matter. They were trespassers and if their bosses hadn't seen fit to inform them of that fact, I would.

'Hand me those bags, Virgil,' I said, and he untied the canvas sacks and handed them over to me.

'I'm going down with you,' Matti said, and for the first time I was so firm with her that she didn't whimper an objection.

'You are not! Virgil, you find a good position and get ready if I need any covering fire.'

He glanced around, said, 'This looks like as good a place as any,' and swung down from his horse. Matti hesitated. I don't know if it was out of fear or stubbornness, but she eventually slipped from the saddle and got down on one knee beside Virgil Sly, rifle at the ready. I had come too far to back down now and so with a loose grin pasted to my lips, I started down to confront the army of railroad workers.

I hated hellfire, but the time for it had come.

8

I saw the heads of the carpenters lift as I walked the bay horse down the sandy bank toward the rock pan where they were working throwing up a depot and what I took to be a storage barn. The word passed from one man to the other, and then — tools fell silent as I approached. A big man with the sleeves of his shirt rolled up came forward to meet me as I halted the horse, my rifle across my saddlebow.

'Help you, mister?' the crew boss asked heavily. He was uncertain what attitude he should adopt. His men were watching him closely. I saw that one of the carpenters had picked up a Winchester from beside a stack of lumber.

'You're on my land,' I said. 'I'll have to ask you to leave.'

'Who the hell are you!' the foreman demanded.

'I just told you. I'm the man who owns the land you're standing on. I don't recall ordering any new construction.'

'You're crazy,' the big man said, looking around him for solidarity. Two or three of the men looked angry, others who had removed their caps to mop their brows just seemed relieved of the chance to take a break. One of them shook his head in amusement.

'I'm not kidding, boys,' I told them. 'I've got riflemen up on the ridge, just waiting for my signal.' They looked that way, seeing Virgil and Matti. At that distance they could not tell that Matti was a woman, but that made no difference anyway.

'Mr Meredith will have something to say about this,' the crew boss said angrily.

'Yes, I suppose he will. But the railroad's plain in the wrong. They've got the wrong building site, and I'm closing it down. You men have your job to do, but I doubt any of you wants to die for it.'

'You're serious, aren't you?' the

foreman said, his eyes narrowing.

'Dead serious. Don't lift that!' I shouted at the man with the Winchester. I shifted my own sights toward him and told him, 'One shot and the guns on the ridge will open up. There'll be a lot of men who don't go home today if that happens.'

'Damn all!' the foreman said unhappily. He tipped back his head, rubbed his eyes and then shrugged. 'I guess you've got the upper hand, mister. Until Meredith hears about this.'

'I guess I have.' I told them, 'You've got ten minutes to pull out. If you can hitch those lumber wagons up in that time, so much the better. You won't be needing them anymore.'

'We'll be back,' a second worker threatened.

'Maybe,' I agreed. But I wasn't planning on leaving them much to come back to. I didn't tell them that, but only watched as they loaded their tools, hitched the horses to the freight wagons and started off, leaving behind a dozen surly glances and a few muttered curses. Breathing out a slow breath of relief, I watched until they had crossed the dry river and then swung down to get to work.

I opened up the canvas sacks to retrieve the two cans Virgil had packed and walked among the framed buildings, splashing coal oil on the new lumber. I kept my eyes moving as I worked, watching for any sign of the men returning. But they were underarmed and under-inclined and I had my watchers on the ridge and I was untroubled at my chore.

Finished, I repacked the two tin cans — we could not afford to replace such things — and dragged a match across my bootheel. It flared and I got to one knee to touch fire to a stream of coal oil. It caught immediately, and in seconds as the flames streaked along the rivulets of spilled fuel, the timbers, new and bone dry from the kiln, caught fire and the sky billowed with dark, wind-tangled clouds of smoke. Saucer-sized flakes of ash twisted upward, driven by the intense heat

The flames rose head-high and then caught the roof joists. The fire writhed against the pale sky, crackling and popping. The bay horse was spooked and I rushed to it, grabbing its reins, swinging aboard to back it from the threatening conflagration. Nothing could have stopped it now. Within minutes the uprights resembled burnt matches and sections of the roofs were collapsing, sending golden sparks up to merge with the crimson flame.

The black, acrid smoke was clouding the sky above me as I guided the bay horse back up the sandy bluff to join Virgil and Matti.

'Well,' Virgil commented laconically, 'that'll get their attention.'

Matti had been watching the destructive growing flames, hands on hips. Now her mouth tightened a little and her eyes met mine. 'If they come after us they'll hit the home ranch first. We'd better get back there. Now.'

The lady was right. I waited for them to mount their horses and then started the bay back toward the Rafter L house, the skies tumultuous and dark behind us.

We rode hard to get there, but approaching the ranch, I already saw four men riding fast toward the house. Bitter with myself for dragging Matti into what looked to be shaping up as a shooting match, I readied my Winchester.

'Hold it, Lang!' Virgil Sly shouted, placing a hand on my wrist. 'Don't that man in front look familiar?'

It took a minute for me to see what Virgil had already observed. The man in front was Bill Forsch, coatless, hatless. I thought at first that the other three were pursuing him, but as they neared the ranch house, I saw that they were riding in a bunch alongside Bill, though I recognized none of them.

'Don't shoot, Lang. One of them is wearing a shield.'

I had already decided to hold my fire,

and I sat the shuddering bay waiting for the lawyer and the three strangers to reach the yard, I glanced at Matti from the corner of my eye. She looked perplexed, determined . . . and beautiful with the flush of the ride on her cheeks.

'It's me, Lang!' Bill Forsch yelled as they reached the ranch yard. He approached on a weary roan horse and we shook hands still on horseback. 'Let me get off this beast,' the lawyer said and he slid from the saddle.

'How in hell did you make it back from Santa Fe so quickly?' I asked, as we stood together, shaking hands once more.

'Nothing to it,' Bill said, still breathing hard. 'I haven't been asleep since the last time you saw me. We broke into the courthouse around midnight, did our snooping and rode back, switching ponies twice on the way. And, Lang, I've got no feeling in my lower half. Have you got a chair — the softer the better?'

'We have. But who are these . . . ?'

'We can talk inside,' Bill said, and he took my arm for support. 'If I can make it that far.'

'Virgil, stand guard,' I said, and helping Bill up onto the porch, we made our way into the house, Matti and the three strangers on our heels.

There were plenty of places to sit down in the over-furnished cabin, but we were practically knee to knee. Both of the men who sat together on one of the yellow settees wore badges, I now saw. United States Marshal's badges. One of the lawmen was tall, narrow with a hawk nose, the other was a small dainty man. Beside Bill Forsch on the other settee sat a round man with the jovial face of an elf. His eyes sparkled with amusement as he studied the house and its quantity of furnishings. I left it to Bill Forsch to take charge. I had no idea what was going on.

'May I introduce Judge Orson Crandall,' Bill said, nodding at the pleasant round man. 'It was only with his assistance that I was able to get into the territorial records office in the middle of the night.' Bill looked at me as he shifted uncomfortably on the cushion. 'Orson, this is Julius Lang himself.'

I thought that was an odd way to introduce me, but I nodded to the judge. Bill went on, 'These are federal marshals, Lang. Coyle and Gere by name. The judge invited them along, thinking they might be needed after I explained matters to him and we had proceeded to research all of the records pertaining to the Rafter L.' I wondered why the territorial judge had been so accommodating. Bill must have dragged him out of bed for this task.

Bill explained, 'Orson and I are old friends.' He glanced at the judge. 'He was once almost my father-in-law.' The lawyer saw my curious glance and said, 'There's a reason I banished myself to Montero. I'll tell you all about it one day.'

Matti couldn't contain herself any

longer. 'What did you find out!' she blurted. Her question was directed at Bill, but Judge Crandall answered.

'Just as Mr Lang surmised,' the judge said, 'the key to the confusion was the missing two hundred acres which he owned and which you, Miss Ullman, on an apparently prior claim, did not. A little digging cleared that up. That two hundred acres, comprising the area known as The Panhandle was transferred to the ownership of Mr Reg Kent *after* the date of Lang's purchase of the land but *before* you came into possession of the property through the will of your uncle.'

'So then . . . ' I began, but the judge raised a pudgy hand to silence me. The taller of the two US marshals continued to study me carefully, his eyes cool and probing.

Judge Crandall continued, 'The bulk of the disputed land which had by then been attached to the Hatchet Ranch was sold less than a month ago to the railroad, the property lying conveniently along the easement and being found suitable for construction of a railhead.'

'Then my deed is no good!' Matti said desolately. She looked at me with tearful blue eyes. 'I never owned the land at all?'

The judge smiled at her. His voice was kind when he answered. 'That, my dear lady, is a finer legal point which Bill and I can untangle when time permits. I can say this, however — Reg Kent certainly does not own that land or any portion of it and his sale of it to the railroad is null and void. The railroad will be served with an immediate cease and desist order.'

Bill, who had seen the smoke roiling into the sky earlier, muttered, 'I think that order has already been served.'

'What's that, Bill?' Judge Crandall inquired.

'Nothing, sir. I believe Mr Lang here was wondering about the railroad's rights concerning any structures that might have been illegally built on his property . . . or Miss Ullman's property.'

'They have no right to reclaim anything of theirs unless Mr Lang is kind enough to offer it,' the judge said strongly. 'In fact he has every right to confiscate or destroy any standing structure as he sees fit.'

'I still don't understand this,' Matti said plaintively. 'Why did Kent go to such lengths, drawing me into this mess as he did?'

Bill thought he could answer. I let him go ahead with an explanation.

'Reg Kent knows Lang. He knew that Lang would never sell out, knew that driving him out would lead to a small war.' Bill smiled faintly. 'Kent has tried that tactic before and come to grief by it. But when Kent learned that the railroad wanted to come through Montero and which route they intended to follow, he became desperate. Lang had to go.

'With the railroad running past, and a railhead virtually adjacent to Kent's property, his cattle could be shipped by the hundreds. No longer would he have to make long grueling cattle drives across the desert to get his cattle to market. Instead of a decimated herd of cattle, they could be held fat and sleek, their full weight on until they were simply loaded aboard the cattle cars. The town of Montero also saw new prosperity ahead. No more dusty desert stagecoaches for potential visitors and buyers. The railroad itself would spend thousands of dollars — '

The front door burst open and Virgil Sly popped in, his face anxious.

'They're coming, Lang! It looks like half the town.'

'Gentlemen?' Judge Crandall said, reaching for his hat without urgency. 'I suggest we adjourn our meeting for the time being.'

We stepped out into the brilliant sunlight, me, the two US marshals, Judge Crandall, Matti and Bill. At first we could see only a boiling cloud of dust moving toward the Rafter L, but in a minute the approaching figures took on form and substance, and we could make them out. Reg Kent rode at the front of the mob, flanked by four of his ranch hands. Just behind them came Alvin Meredith. Mayor Jefferson shared the buggy he was driving. Judge Plank and the banker, Rufus Potter, rode beside them, and then in a surging, angry knot came, as Virgil had indicated, what seemed to be half the town of Montero.

'Well, well,' the judge said in an unconcerned voice. 'What sort of armed insurrection have we here? Bill, identify these ringleaders for me, would you.'

Bill was still doing that, pointing out the various officials and instigators of the mob as Reg Kent drew his gray horse up roughly and was preparing to level a snarling order at me. The sight of the judge cautioned the rancher, the two armed men wearing badges caused him to fall mute. He looked around anxiously for help. There was, I saw, a legal paper of some kind in his hand — the bill of sale for the Panhandle, I assumed.

'What's all this!' Mayor Jefferson managed to roar as he stepped from the buggy he had been driving. Judge Plank whispered something urgently to him. Plank, himself, straightened his vest and extended a hand to Judge Crandall.

'Sir! This is a privilege. What brings you to our fair town?'

'Oh, I think you know,' Crandall said affably. 'Why don't we all discuss this matter — after you have turned your band of thugs away? They are trespassing, and I would hate to see the result if they persist in this behavior.'

It was the mayor who returned on foot to halt the mass of approaching men, who, stirred up by anger, or simply having been offered free liquor and a morning's entertainment, waited in a sullen group.

'Say the word, Judge Crandall,' one of the marshals, the tall one, Coyle said, 'and I'll disperse this mob.' I glanced at the man, the calm intent in his eyes, and half-believed that he could do it.

'No, Marshal Coyle,' Crandall answered

with a chuckle, 'I don't believe that will be necessary now. The mayor is explaining their mistake to them.'

'Look here,' Alvin Meredith said. The railroad boss was beside himself with rage. 'I demand to know what is going on here!'

'You have been swindled,' Judge Crandall told him simply. 'I suggest any further discussion concerning this business be taken up with Mr Kent and resolved by your attorneys. That is,' he added, 'if I do not decide to arrest Mr Kent here and now.'

Meredith was so angry he was sputtering now. 'This man,' he said leveling a finger at me, 'has destroyed thousands of dollars' worth of railroad property.'

'Are you referring to the illegally built structures erected on Mr Lang's land?' Judge Crandall asked pleasantly. 'He had every right to do as he pleased with that property, sir. Count yourself lucky that the railhead was not completed and a train stopped there. No,' the judge said, holding up a hand as Alvin Meredith started in again. 'No more discussion of the matter. The rest is between you and Kent and your legal people. Press whatever charges you wish against him, that's up to you.'

Seeing he was beaten, Meredith spun on his heel and stalked away fuming, sparing one last searing glance at Reg Kent who had crumpled up the useless bill of sale in his hand and dropped it to the earth.

The mob had begun to disperse, making its unruly way back toward Montero by the time Mayor Jefferson returned, puffing and sweating with the exertion. Judge Crandall had a few words for him — and for Judge Plank.

'You are an elected official, Mayor Jefferson, and since no one has as yet implicated you in any criminal acts, I can do nothing but publicly rebuke you. And wish you luck on being re-elected when your backers to whom you have promised a railroad spur and its concomitant prosperity discover it was

190

all a pipe dream.' He turned then to Judge Plank.

'You, however, are an appointee to your position, Plank. I intend to see that you are replaced immediately. I have an honest young attorney in mind to succeed you.' He looked meaningfully at Bill Forsch.

'Now I'll never get out of Montero,' Bill moaned.

The meeting went on like that for only a few more minutes, with Rufus Potter complaining that I had drained the town marshal's fund in a matter of a few days, Plank continuing to plead for mercy and the mayor looking sick.

In the meantime Marshal Coyle had eased up beside me, those black eyes of his searching. Matti was near enough to overhear his throttled words, and so was Virgil Sly. 'Socorro, wasn't it, Lang? We had a temporary deputy by the same name down that way, looked kind of like you, too. We had a man convicted of murder in custody waiting for the hangman when this Lang let the prisoner escape, claiming he was innocent.'

'Was he?' I asked.

'He was,' Coyle affirmed. 'Three days after this man — this drifter named Sly — was to have been executed, the real murderer gave himself up.'

'Fortunate for Sly,' I said innocently.

'Still,' Coyle said expressionlessly, 'we don't like rogue marshals who take the law into their own hands. There might still be charges against Lang pending in Socorro.'

I glanced at Virgil Sly, looked away and then commented, 'Let's hope that the man has enough sense, then, to stay miles away from Socorro.'

'You think he will?' Coyle asked quietly.

'I'd bet on it.'

Coyle walked away and Matti's attention returned to the legal problems at hand. She approached Judge Crandall who was slowly lighting a cigar as he listened thoughtfully to Plank's last plea and shook his head in refusal, leaving Plank to plod away, planning his next career.

'Sir?' Matti said and Crandall turned his elfin eyes on her. 'You still haven't made it clear. Does this land belong to me or to Lang? Am I a squatter, or does he now own two hundred acres of my property!' She was frustrated, and rightly so. The judge put a gentle hand on her shoulder.

'I haven't had time to review all of the facts, or to consider the conflicting claims in depth, let alone make a decision. This is a matter for the local judiciary, anyway. I am certain that the newly appointed Judge Forsch will be able to sort it all out in a fair and impartial manner.'

Matti turned her big blue eyes on Bill Forsch; Bill glanced at me. He shook his head and said somewhat cryptically:

'It would have been easier just to marry her.'

9

'Look what I found!' Virgil Sly sang out, and we looked up to see him carrying a white-faced calf across the withers of his blue roan. The small animal bawled and rolled its big brown eyes at us. Matti got up from her porch chair and went to help lower the calf to the ground. She crouched beside it and stroked its curly reddish coat.

'Is this the one that was missing all that time?' Matti asked Virgil.

'That's him, Matti. He couldn't find the herd again, but he wandered up right over there beyond the water tank. He was good and lost, but he knew where home was.'

Matti looked up at me, her smile bright and meaningful. Yes, we knew where home was too, both of us. Right here, on *our* land. Bill Forsch had made a some-what confusing decision concerning the property that neither Matti nor I fully understood, couched as it was in legal language. What Bill explained was that we had joint tenancy in perpetuity. None of which mattered at all after Bill, in his new judge's robes married Matti and me in his chambers fifteen minutes after the case was settled. We were now going to have to share everything in perpetuity. The decision concerning the land meant nothing in the end.

Bill told me that Clarence Applewhite had recovered fully under Mama Fine's care, and that Cal was gentleman enough not to laugh out loud when they had approached him about the possibility of him staying on as permanent town marshal.

The day was clouding up. The air was fresher, cooler. When it rained this time it would not be a dust-rain, but a real out and out cloudburst if we were to judge by the thunderheads massing over Arapaho Peak.

Matti continued to fuss over the calf,

leading it to water, currying it as it drank. I tipped my hat back and sauntered toward the lean-to to see to my horse. I glanced again at the unfinished addition to the house, proud of what I had accomplished so far. Lumber was a drug on the market just then. Reg Kent had no use for the stockpile he had accumulated — not where the territory had sent him to do his time, and the railroad had balked at paying to ship all of their material back to Santa Fe. Those who wanted lumber in Montero could afford it just then — even us, and so I was determined to expand the tiny cabin so that Matti would have enough room to keep all of the things she had brought from San Francisco that meant so much to her.

The gusting wind followed me and a few heavy drops of rain began to fall, pocking the sandy soil. The sorrel seemed glad to see me. Its eyes brightened and it swiveled its ears as if waiting for me to speak. Perhaps the horse had been trying to warn me, I don't know, all I know is that I neither heard nor saw him coming until it was too late.

Cheyenne Baker stepped out from the shadowed corner of the lean-to and stood facing me, legs braced, his hand hovering near his holstered Colt revolver. He looked gaunter than I remembered him, trail-dusty and disheveled. His eyes were bright and deadly. His thin lips barely moved when he challenged me.

'I told you I'd kill you, Lang. Way back when you shot me up and threw me in that cell. That's why I'm here. I'm a man who lives up to his promises.'

I thought about everything that I had going for me now, about the way the ranch was building up, about Matti! I could not die now, shot down by this wild-eyed gunman. Not now!

'Calm down, Cheyenne,' I said quietly. 'It won't be worth it. Not really. You've gotten away from the law — everyone thinks you died out there on the desert after the jail break. You don't have to worry about hanging, about being arrested. You can live free. No one needs to know that Cheyenne Baker is still alive.'

'I do, Lang,' he said menacingly. 'Don't you get it? A man like you, I would think you would understand. Let everyone think I died like a dog out on the desert! No, Lang. Let them know that Cheyenne Baker will claw his way back out of his grave to even the score with a man who has wronged him.'

He went for his gun then and I threw myself to one side as his bullet whipped past my ear. The sorrel, startled by the near explosion of the gun reared up and side-stepped away, trying to toss its tether. Cheyenne tried to bull his way around the horse's flanks for a second shot, but I had dropped to one knee and drawn my own Colt. As he settled his sights on me again, I fired.

The roar of the revolver was like close thunder. The bullet ripped through Cheyenne Baker's throat, and I rose to watch him crumple up and fall to the hay-strewn earth to die. Matti's scream was terrible as she rushed to me, Virgil carrying his rifle close behind her. Matti threw herself into my arms and I held her a long minute, grateful for her soft, close comfort. Virgil toed the dead man and grunted.

'Cheyenne Baker. I never thought we'd see him again.'

'We won't this time,' I said. 'We'll lower him down into a grave so deep he won't be able to crawl out of it.'

★ ★ ★

Matti and I sat our horses on the ridge overlooking the Panhandle. Whipsaw Creek was running full and fast and wide following the rain.

'There really is a creek here,' she said in a kind of wonder, as the white-water river boiled past.

'Now and then. This time of year the water collects in the hills, gathers its force in the canyons and roars through the valley. It's a wonderful sight to see when it happens. All that providence spreading across the land, greening the grass, bringing those dead willows and cottonwoods into bud almost overnight.'

'A land determined not to die,' Matti said. The wind twisted her reddish hair, shifting it across her wide blue eyes, but she did not brush it aside, only watched the river run.

'Lang?' she said with a playful smile.

'Yes?'

'You are speaking of the grass greening, the trees coming back to life, all nurtured by the rainfall. Do you suppose . . . if we found just the right place along the creek, where it ponds up in the dry season . . . if we were to plant it carefully and nurture it through the hard times . . .

'Do you think a walnut tree would grow here?'

We do hope that you have enjoyed reading this large print book.

Did you know that all of our titles are available for purchase?

We publish a wide range of high quality large print books including:
Romances, Mysteries, Classics
General Fiction
Non Fiction and Westerns

Special interest titles available in large print are:
The Little Oxford Dictionary
Music Book, Song Book
Hymn Book, Service Book

Also available from us courtesy of Oxford University Press:
Young Readers' Dictionary
(large print edition)
Young Readers' Thesaurus
(large print edition)

For further information or a free brochure, please contact us at:
Ulverscroft Large Print Books Ltd.,
The Green, Bradgate Road, Anstey,
Leicester, LE7 7FU, England.
Tel: (00 44) **0116 236 4325**
Fax: (00 44) **0116 234 0205**

HELL'S COURTYARD

Cobra Sunman

Indian Territory, popularly called Hell's Courtyard, was where bad men fled to escape the law. Buck Rogan, a deputy marshal hunting the killer Jed Calder, found the trail leading into Hell's Courtyard and went after his quarry, finding every man's hand against him. Rogan was also searching for the hideout of Jake Yaris, an outlaw running most of the lawlessness directed at Kansas and Arkansas. Single-minded and capable, Rogan would fight the bad men to the last desperate shot.

57002